The Philanthropist

Adrian Cattermole

 iUniverse

The Philanthropist

iUniverse books may be ordered through booksellers or by contacting:

iUniverse
1663 Liberty Drive
Bloomington, IN 47403
www.iuniverse.com
1-800-Authors (1-800-288-4677)

Because of the dynamic nature of the Internet, any web addresses or
links contained in this book may have changed since publication and
may no longer be valid. The views expressed in this work are solely those
of the author and do not necessarily reflect the views of the publisher,
and the publisher hereby disclaims any responsibility for them.

Any people depicted in stock imagery provided by Thinkstock are
models, and such images are being used for illustrative purposes only.
Certain stock imagery © Thinkstock.

ISBN: 978-1-4917-7908-8 (sc)
ISBN: 978-1-4917-7909-5 (e)

Library of Congress Control Number: 2015918512

Print information available on the last page.

iUniverse rev. date: 11/10/2015

Contents

Britain

He became known as 'The Philanthropist'. Simple as that – 'The Philanthropist'. Nobody really knew his name though many guessed. (Wrongly as it turned out - even if some of the fingered, denying, but maybe without enough forceful authority, enjoyed their brief spell of celebrity before sentiment moved swiftly onto another name.) And so 'The Philanthropist' he became - just one more alias to add to the list. Many simply did not believe he existed at all; conspiracy theorists had a field day. Was it just a made-up idea, a good-news story to divert our attention away from the latest Government shenanigans? Was it all a ruse to sell newspapers, heaven knows there had been many before this? Was the anonymity a cover for some Corporation looking to surprise us all with their generosity? Was it all a con anyway? Nobody knew. All they knew was that somebody; let us too call him 'The Philanthropist', was making surprise gifts at an alarming rate.

At first the press loved the idea of some modern day Robin Hood, doling out largesse left, right and centre. It was almost as good as the lottery. And though his gifts were always unannounced most of the recipients simply couldn't resist their fifteen seconds of fame, causing a veritable media circus as reporters sped across the country from one lucky family to another. And so it became the most popular of stories, wiping tornadoes and politics and scandals from the front pages. For a while. Until the sniping started. 'Who decided just who the deserving poor actually were?' 'Why should some receive and others be denied?' 'Who gave him the right to give his money away in this fashion?' 'Who was this mystery person anyway?'

A man, surely! 'The Philanthropist' must be a man, as only a man could have garnered such wealth in the first place, besides a woman would have sought out more publicity, or so the editorials (written, you guessed, by men) all agreed. But why the mystery, why the subterfuge, why no name? Everyone wanted to know his name, yet no-one had a clue. And even the guesses were way off the mark. Nobody was really sure what he was up to, were his actions purely altruistic? Or was there a deeper more sinister motive? What had motivated such largesse? And had he paid his taxes on what must have been an immense fortune? Eventually questions were asked in Parliament.

"Did the Prime Minister know the identity of the mystery benefactor? Did she approve of his (or possibly her) actions? Why did the authorities not know who 'The Philanthropist' was? Was National Security in any way being threatened by this irrational behaviour?"

All to no avail; "Our Government will strive to unravel the complex web of companies set up by and popularly known as 'The Philanthropist Foundation'" and "Yes, no stone will be left unturned to establish the identity of 'The Philanthropist' and the legality, not only of the monies dispersed, but the very nature of the gifts themselves."

But the Government were as helpless as the rest of us. The various companies accounts all appeared to be audited and in perfect order, but it was like a four dimensional maze, an ever changing Rubik's cube with layers of complexity mired in ever more confusing detail; this company was owned by that one, which was in turn owned partially by others, mostly offshore, some in territories it was not easy or even possible to obtain details from. The Directors changed with amazing regularity and were mostly now untraceable, companies closed and were taken over by others with bewildering speed and no-one could actually pin any individual down. Hapless Accountants and Auditors smiled for the cameras but knew very little. But yes, the correct tax appeared to be paid on all these companies where they fell under the jurisdiction of Her Majesties Tax Inspectors. Enquiries were ongoing but so far no actual wrong doing could be found at all. So why were people so upset? Was it simply down to jealousy? Was it the fact that this was such an unorthodox method of helping people? Where was the accountability? Who had decided who should be rewarded? And why not simply give them money, for goodness sake? There was nothing wrong with charity (we all gave where we could), but this was on a ridiculous scale. And it had silently crept up on us; it was a few years before we began to understand the complexity or indeed the scale of the gifts. And by then the thing was colossal, an immense undertaking, and by its nature almost incomprehensible. And so 'The Philanthropist' was created and even if his existence, his actual persona, was questioned there was no mistake about the gifts he was dispersing.

The Government were made to look rather stupid; they were, after all, the champions of free-enterprise, of allowing people to do exactly what they wanted with their own money. But this giving away of such vast sums went against all commonsense; it almost insulted one's intelligence. This was not how things were meant to work; the invisible hand of the free market was supposed to regulate everything, but these irresponsible actions had thrown the entire market into chaos. And even the Opposition were furious; redistributing wealth was the job of Government not of Charity. Who gave an individual the power to decide who was to be helped? Where was the fairness, where the means testing? People were seemingly picked at random; no proper records were being kept. How could the tax system possibly be expected to work with this almighty spanner thrown into the works? All the normal rules of

Government were being turned upside down. But try as they might neither side could find anything actually illegal in it.

And still no-one knew who The Philanthropist was, or why he had done it, and despite widespread hostility appeared to be still continuing, though at a much slower pace, to give away his fortune. No-one knew quite how he had managed it, or just as worrying how he had acquired the money in the first place. There were wild speculations as to how much he had spent. Three hundred billion? One trillion? Even trying to guess was complicated by markets crashing and currencies fluctuating as a result of his actions. The best educated guess was about six hundred billion pounds; an enormous sum of money by any reckoning. Far more than any Government was spending anywhere in the world to alleviate poverty, or in fact all of them combined; nowhere near in fact. Who had that sort of money in the first place? Had it been borrowed? But no, the banks insisted they had never financed any of the companies which made up 'The Foundation'. It was a complete mystery. Were the Chinese behind it all, trying to destabilise the country? Or the Russians maybe - you could never trust those bastards.

On paper it looked like a pure act of philanthropy by a private individual or maybe a small group of like minded people. But no-one knew who, there were no leaks at all, no-one was talking. It was a huge secret but it all seemed legal and above board. Just incredibly absurd. But it had caused the biggest re-distribution of wealth ever known. Many reporters tried to discover who The Philanthropist was, how he had amassed his fortune and more importantly why he gave it all away. I have managed to uncover most of the story, though some elements eluded even me; at times it was like trying to nail water to a wall, as soon as I felt I had him pinned down he would slip silkily through my fingers. A part of me was reluctant to tell this story, maybe I had begun to like him, admire him even, but as you will discover he was not exactly the nicest of people. ...

Suffolk

The Philanthropist or the person who would later transform himself into The Philanthropist was born in the very early nineteen-fifties, in a small town in Suffolk; even his birth, though I have seen his birth certificate, seems as lepidopterean as the man himself. He has trans-mutated so many times that even I find it hard to be certain. His true identity (and yes he was a man) hardly matters now, as he has been able to change his name many times, taking on and buying new identities when needed, and chameleon-like managing to blend in to his new background almost unnoticed. He is a different person entirely now from the one he was as a boy. But as a snail leaves a slimy trail behind and hides hoping no-one can see him safe in his shell, so despite his best efforts The Philanthropist too has left a very faint but smudgy trail. For those like me who knew where to look his beginnings were strangely ordinary. Remarkably he has managed to live quite outside the law and yet has appeared to conform wherever possible. Many times he has disappeared only to pop up in another guise, another name, another company, another country even. His secret is that he has never discussed his plans with anyone at all. Nobody was ever his confidante, no-one has ever guessed his true identity and nobody ever knew the extent of his wealth or where it all came from. But he did exist. I have found out that much, and yet the man himself keeps eluding me; it is as if the more I learn about him the less I know. His grand idea came upon him gradually, crystallising into an actual plan slowly as he limped from one persona to another. At times I have thought him to be the most unhappy of individuals but in fact as he looked back on a complex life and though he has practically ceased his philanthropic activities and rumour has it that he has simply run out of money, he had never been happier. Mission accomplished.

As a child the philanthropist was much like other children, no-one marked him out as in any way special. He was bright, clever without being particularly brilliant, and for a while a diligent if unremarkable student. But something in him began to stir and about the time he was nine or ten he started to disobey. Not openly, but on the sly. He gained great satisfaction from getting away with things, and when nobody ever found out then even better. The fact that only he knew what he had done was the best feeling in the world, everyone else carried on oblivious to his actions – only he knew what he had achieved.

He would steal fellow student's notebooks (he was the class monitor and had the responsibility of collecting homework for teacher) and locking himself in the lavatory during break would meticulously cull all the best answers, being careful to subtly change the wording so no-one would find him out. He rose to the top of the class without appearing to be that clever at all. In fact he could have easily answered the questions himself but stealing his way to the top felt far more rewarding; a cleverer way of being clever, if you like.

He even became a real thief, but he never got caught because he never left the shop with the goods. On a Saturday morning in the tiny Co-op food store, he would take a chocolate bar from the sweet counter, sliding it into the sleeve of his school blazer, and while no-one was looking secrete it behind the birthday cards or in the ice-cream fridge, at the same time as removing a Choc-Ice and placing it still frozen but bound to cause a lovely mess in the coat pocket of some old lady who was busy deciding which biscuits to buy. He was quietly re-arranging the world around him, a habit he would return to time and time again. No-one knew he was in control, that it was he who was subtly changing the ordered world he was forced to live in. At home tins of spam were mysteriously found behind the washing soda under the sink, flower-pots kept turning themselves upside down in the shed, his father's bike chain would come undone as soon as he put his foot on the pedal, and the lid of the toothpaste tin seemed to be welded shut (but I only used it myself this morning, father). And his parents did sometimes question him, in an offhand way, but his look of bemused innocence was so sincere that they never really suspected him (such a good boy) of such silly and unexplained misdemeanours. He was clever too, he never repeated a trick if questioned about it, they just became one-off mysteries; his parents even laughed about there being a ghost in the house. There was no ghost, no poltergeist at all - just a small boy who quietly rearranged things, but this secret perpetrator derived immense satisfaction from these tiny and some might think pointless acts of deception.

And he told no-one. He was living in his own world most of the time, an inner world of plans and ideas far removed from the one he conformed to. His parents did think he was a bit strange, he would spend hours upstairs in his bedroom when other kids were running around the streets shouting and letting off steam.

"What is he doing up there? He should be outside, playing with the other kids." his father would ask, to which his mother might reply "Reading I think, he is always reading these days. He's got books all over his bedroom."

And he was reading. He would not only borrow books from the library, but also bought second hand books at jumble sales by the shelf-full (sixpence the lot sonny, do you need a bag?). He worked his way through detective stories, Simenon and Agatha Christie, and novels by the dozen, but his favourites by far were History, he couldn't get enough of History. Working out where things had gone wrong. He loved the fact that History was more than anything a litany of mistakes, steps too far, blunders and wrong turnings that always ended in failure. He relished the mistakes, the downfall, the collapse of Empires, the overthrow of Kings and Tyrants; the sad defeats of political leaders. Sitting upstairs as the strains of the Nine O Clock News wafted up the carpeted stairs he would rub his hands together as another Stuart died.

His father might bemoan and secretly regret not being close enough to kick a ball about with him, but secretly his mother was pleased; he was so well behaved, not like those council house kiddies in the estate down the road, so naughty and dirty and rude. Not like her son, he was different, but then she prided herself that *they* were different. They lived in their own house, a semi-detached three bedroom house in a nice quiet street, a long way away from those council houses that had sprung up everywhere since the War. They had inherited it from her parents who had bought it for next to nothing in the thirties and then conveniently died leaving it to their only daughter. But still it put them a step higher on the ladder, hardly anyone owned their own houses, only Doctors and Teachers and Lawyers and the like. So what if Bert's friends at his work (he had joined the lawn-mower factory at fourteen and hoped to retire there one day) thought them posh, they were only jealous. Yes, they only had the one child; she had had complications during the pregnancy and was warned not to risk having more children, so the one boy would have to do. A relief in a way, and he was such a good boy too, never caused them any trouble at all.

Good? Well yes, on the surface, but subversive he definitely was too. He had a paper round and once mixed-up (on purpose) and delivered old Mr. Stanhope's copy of Tit-Bits to the spinster sisters Jones who lived three doors away. He was contrite and full of apologies and was duly forgiven and told to be more careful in future and Mr Stanhope was kindly asked to come in and collect his magazine from the shop in future. Nobody suspected he had done it on purpose - well it was an easy mistake to make. He had been quietly re-arranging the world. The less he was suspected the greater his sense of achievement.

One day he went in by bus to Ipswich and walked to the second-hand bookshop where he had heard that if you asked the man behind the counter you could obtain a copy of 'Lady Chatterley's Lover' that wasn't available in W. H. Smiths. He handed over his five shillings and tucked the infamous book inside his blazer. He wasn't excited at all by the notorious passages; he wanted the book for a different purpose altogether. In the secrecy of his bedroom and with a razor blade he carefully excised the passages with the rude words on them. Next morning his father, face full of soap, was furious that his blade had gone missing; it was there yesterday he could swear. At church that Sunday he retained his hymn book and upstairs in his bedroom he pasted the offending passages over 'All things bright and beautiful" a regular favourite. He had to wait a few weeks before the hymn was chosen, and as the organist started playing our hero almost pee-ed himself with the secret knowledge that someone, he had no idea who, would innocently open their hymn book and be confronted with a different purple headed mountain than the one everyone else was singing about. He resisted the temptation to look round the cold and stony walls to see who was blushing, an elderly mother or a young father maybe, or just as possibly an old spinster closing the book in disgust, or maybe a young man even secreting it themselves to read later. He gripped the wooden pew, excited but still singing along, another victory gained. The knowledge that he had done it was enough for him, re-arranging the world once again.

Some mornings he would steal one inner double page of 'The Times' or 'The Telegraph' and folding it into a tiny square would read the articles while appearing to be assiduously studying his text-book, as the maths teacher was droning on and on, Pythagoras' theory being scratched on the blackboard. Some outraged customer might complain or more likely tut-tut as they skipped over the missing pages, but he got away with it for months until one day he stopped simply out of boredom. Strangely he was very good at maths, even though he had been reading of Rhodesia and UDI or a speech Enoch Powell was making rather than learning about parallelograms or logarithms. Somehow he absorbed it all, he understood maths; it was simple, it was logical. Numbers always added up, numbers were finite; numbers never let you down and already at twelve he knew almost instinctively that people always would.

Every morning he put his cheek up to his mother to be kissed, even when he was fourteen and in long trousers at last. But secretly he despised her; with her unbounded belief in him and her cloying love too. Why couldn't she see through him? He saw through her. He saw through everybody – it was all hypocrisy, and he despised her for her simplicity and her unconditional love and her insipid goodness. And him too, his father - of course he despised them both. What was there not to despise? They were normal, they were small-minded, parochial; they had no grand ambitions at all. Avoiding embarrassment and keeping their heads beneath the parapet were the two driving forces of their tiny lives. They had taught him one thing only. Never to be like them, never to be victims of the system, never to simply accept that change was that which was forced upon you but to be the instigator of change himself. He knew he was different, that he would succeed where all around him he saw failure; his schoolmates were failures before they even got started, sure to repeat the mistakes of their parents; the teachers were failures (ending up passing on pointless so-called 'knowledge' rather than doing something interesting with their lives) but most of all his parents; a housewife constantly cleaning and cooking and his father a factory worker, more machine himself than man. He was determined to be different from them.

And worse of all they loved him. He gave nothing in return and still they worshipped him, even his father would tousle his hair when he came in from work and would try to engage him, though the boy showed no interest in football at all. He longed to escape their claustrophobic love, to live an untrammelled life, disengaged from all this pointless sentimentality. But that was for the future, for now he was happy to play the game; content in the knowledge that it was all a game. He smiled when his mother kissed him; an embarrassed teenage smile, but a smile nonetheless. He nodded back a greeting to his father when he came into the room, to have ignored him might seem churlish, and despite his secret loathing he was always polite. Politeness was his calling card, the one he hid his smirk behind. It was all a game, all of this life, school, parents; the life they all lived was just a stupid game. As he looked around at his classmates he realised that none of them even knew they were in the game at all; he was the only one conscious that he was playing the game. He was the only one who even suspected that it was a game. He knew-and was playing by his own rules too. And he knew that though all of life was a game, he was destined to be a winner.

He had no illusions about love. Parental love that is, but he knew that 'love' was the key to unlocking the gates of lust. Like all young men he was horny as hell, and would sometimes, while 'sorting his papers out' at seven in the morning, loosen the staple in Men Only and gently ease out and remove the centrefold, careful not to tear her. No-one ever complained that this was missing but he would tape the page up on the back of the toilet door while pretending to have a touch of diarrhoea and wank to his heart's content. Carefully unpeeling and refolding his precious be-bosomed ladies he would pull a face of embarrassed discomfort as his mother questioned him about what on earth he had been eating at school. Promising to stay away from the tuck-shop he would later sell the still neatly folded pictures for sixpence a time to his jealous classmates.

He went to the church youth club, played table tennis and hung around with the other teenage kids, posing just like them but not like them at all; he alone knew it was all a pose. He even went to the pub a few times though alcohol did nothing for him; he didn't even like the taste. He had a couple of 'girlfriends', snogging in the darkened alley behind the church his hands would roam and explore. He knew the girls he was kissing were real and not the statuesque un-breathing models in Men Only but he was quite surprised at the way breasts were soft and yet firm at the same time. The nipples even were pliable and rubbery under his fingers. Amazing. You would never have guessed from those glossy perky photo's that they were so warm and soft and comforting. One time his fingers strayed down to the waistband of Mary Ash's knickers and he was suddenly full of apprehension. She was slightly older than him, almost nineteen and rumour had it that she was, well let's just say, generous with her favours. As the backs of his fingers gently edged along the elastic she drew in her breath and whispered into his ear "Outside only, don't put your hand inside my knickers."

He slowly drew his fingers away, circling her belly before changing direction and slipping it again to the comfort of her breasts, ripe under her loosened brassiere. She had spoiled the moment. Her complicity, her admittance that she knew what he was thinking, had upset him. He had been in his own world up to that point. The fact that Mary Ash was a real person with real feelings hadn't really occurred to him until that moment. He had been the instigator, the secret navigator, drawing the contours of her body on the map in his mind. He had been in control; he hadn't asked permission to touch her. Don't be silly – no-one asked a girl's permission. You attacked by stealth, searching your way blindly and slowly gaining inch by inch tiny pieces of territory, and if she said nothing then all the better. She wasn't stupid, she must know what he was after, and she was enjoying the thrill as much as he was, he in seeing just how far he could go, and she in daring herself to see just how far she would let him go. And nothing was ever said. This was not a negotiation but a shared and silent adventure for both of them. The boy did all the running, the nudging at the barriers but the girl was the one who knew where the limits lay, or might be extended a fraction this time. And it was all unsaid, that was the best of it, it was all implied, subtly accepted as the way things were without any discussion.

But Mary's implicit acceptance that she knew what he was doing had spoiled the moment for him, or rather her speaking; her acknowledging of his own thoughts had caused him to pause. To continue he would have to accept that she was a party to it, a willing party rather than a dumb object for him to secretly examine. She had disturbed the moment, that exquisite moment when he had first touched the elastic waistband of a girl's knickers, the anticipation would never be quite the same again, that moment of unknowing, the remote possibility of touching a girl's cunt (even on the outside of blue serge knickers), that measured moment was gone. He knew if he put his hand back that he would be allowed to feel what he had only before imagined as tightly curled hair and compressed folds – but outside only, he couldn't put his fingers inside.

Not that he really wanted to. Not yet. He was still learning, still mapping out the beauty, still enjoying every stealthily gained contour of a girl's body. This was in the pre-pornography sixties; gynaecological explicitness was not yet available, all you had was a basic line drawing in an encyclopaedia, a modicum of playground information and your imagination. Magazines like Men Only or Playboy never featured full-frontal shots, just bums and tits. And even Heath and Efficiency, the nudist magazine, only had blurry black and white pictures that even under a magnifying glass told you nothing at all. Maybe it was better that way, it slowed things down, scared you a bit too. Not that it dampened your enthusiasm, sharpened it perhaps. But her half-invitation, half acceptance that she was giving her permission had killed any desire he might have had. He resumed his kissing of her, his tongue pushing harder and harder into her mouth, angrily pushing her tongue away while one hand hung fist clenched by her side and the other ferociously squeezed her breast. As she sighed at his apparent passion and almost swooned under his mouth he felt disgusted with both himself and her. Why had she spoken, why had she entered into his private thoughts, why had she broken through the silent exploration he was enjoying. Though he had gone further with her than any girl before - he finished with Mary Ash a week later.

He never fell in 'love' with any of the girls he met, at school or youth club. And he only had a few girlfriends; he was the one who usually ended it, he was never sure why. It was when they started showing signs of emotion, when he felt they were starting to become attached to him. If only he could kiss and touch them with no returning reaction. And this love everyone talked about, he couldn't understand that at all. Maybe his rejection and ridiculing of his parents love stopped him from feeling this most common of human emotions. They say that before you can love others you must learn to love yourself. He wasn't even sure if he liked himself, he certainly didn't like anyone else.

This didn't stop him becoming obsessed by a few of the girls he saw; and one or two became objects of almost insatiable desire. Their very untouchable lack of attainment, the remoteness of ever consummating his passion became a source of intense and sharp pleasure in his secret hours as he tried to recreate the hidden essence of them. Laying in the dark, his hand round his throbbing cock he would conjure up the essence of them, the almost imperceptible rise and fall of a tiny bosom, the swirl of hairs on their forearms, the way they smiled, the way they laughed at his feeble jokes. He worshipped them, but as objects not people; he didn't want to talk to them, he just wanted to look at them, to somehow possess them without their knowledge at all. At school he would stand behind them in the dinner queue just trying to get the merest whisper of body odour from them, or the gentle heft of their hair if he leaned forward and let it touch his face as he greedily inhaled the sweaty dankness hidden in those tresses. His hands, merely inches away from the rise of their bottoms in those pretty summer smocks, would almost tremble in anticipatory ecstasy. But he never touched them. They never knew. He never let them know they were the objects of his veneration. This was his secret pleasure, his alone. He couldn't risk them ever guessing, ever reciprocating; that would have spoiled everything. He never fell in love with them; they were objects of perfection to be worshipped, adored but never realised. Or often just one part of them was to be worshipped, those strands of hair that strayed so carelessly on the back of their necks, the gentle swell of those breasts straining against the thin white blouse, or the curve of that calf, the imagined line of those thighs under thin poplin dresses, the way they walked with the merest of sashays would be enough for him to admire at a distance. Other boys would boast of sexual conquest, of actually doing it sometimes, but The Philanthropist was never jealous. He knew that his pleasure, his sharp secret excitement was far greater, far more intense than any possibly imagined by those other boys. In fact he knew beyond certainty that his was the only intelligence worth consideration, his appreciation of beauty the only true feeling, his knowledge of the world superior to all others.

Though 'love' for girls, for his parents, in fact for anyone at all, eluded him he did fall deeply in love with Music. The Beatles were his first true love, and he fell headlong for them. They were safe, he would never meet them, the only meeting was in his appreciation of their music; the music they had created specifically for him. He dismissed Beatlemania as some sort of superficial nonsense, none of those so-called fans had any real appreciation, none of them understood the Beatles in the way he did. None of these screaming girls understood that they were singing just for him. He had a tape-recorder, a large reel to reel machine which his father had bought him second-hand but in perfect condition one Christmas. He befriended older boys who might have their records and taped them along with Top of the Pops each week. He would spend hours replaying these tapes up in his bedroom, rewinding and writing the words out time and again until they made sense. He would cut pictures from newspapers and magazines of the Fab four and draw them in biro over and over on sketch pads. He liked the hard edge of the biro, and would shade in eyebrows and pupils to a dark dense blue and try to make the pen just graze the page to suggest the edge of a nose or a chin. He had always been quite good at drawing faces, though not from memory. He liked to try to replicate the essence of a look or an emotion from a photograph, he knew he couldn't draw from real life, in Art lesson he never tried but give him a photo and he could capture something that even the camera hadn't managed to reveal. He filled up sketch book after sketch book with images of his heroes, but he never took them into school or even showed his parents. These were for his eyes only; this was a love affair he was conducting completely for himself alone. The fact that he would never meet his heroes didn't matter in the slightest. He wasn't interested in them as real people. It was their image, the recorded music they made, the photos, the projection of their personalities that he was in love with. Some might call it obsession but that was because they simply had no conception what they were sharing, him and the Beatles – at one against the world. He hung on their every word, sung or spoken and as they drifted into weirder territory, he duly followed. No-one could understand or appreciate the special relationship that was going on in his mind.

As the sixties progressed he got swept up in the whole youth culture thing, the hippies, psychedelia, bells and flowers in your hair and he too dreamed of going to San Francisco and hanging out with The Byrds or The Grateful Dead. That was the life he craved, being stoned (though he could only imagine what drugs might be like) and listening to music all day, becoming absorbed in the music, obliterating everything else, hung up on an everlasting guitar note, just living for the moment – that was what he desired. He would listen to Caroline or Radio Luxemburg into the small hours with his transistor radio under the covers with him, the music lulling him into and waking him from a fitful slumber. He was living for the music only. It was his escape, his private Nirvana, his secret place. Alone with his music he could block out the real world, cut out everything else. He sought and found oblivion in the pure noise of music, it became his new obsession. He stopped closely watching and drinking in the essence of girls and drifted into the sublime sounds of his favourite guitar bands. He knew it was only a matter of time now before he left Suffolk behind and came to London where his real life would begin. He had known since his very early teens that he would leave Suffolk far behind him, and London was his desired location. Another obsession; as he read all he could find about the place.

But before then he needed to find out how to be good. Being good became another obsession. And he saw no discrepancy between being good and his obvious small misdemeanours, his secret re-arranging of the material world. His mother had a framed photograph of 'Jesus' and a 'Lifeboy'. Of course it was not actually Jesus, but a man dressed as Jesus, or what we all thought Jesus looked like, white robes, long hair and beard and a real painted-in halo. He would stare at the picture as a young boy and want to be that Lifeboy, or maybe Jesus himself, he was never quite sure. Maybe he was Jesus but nobody had realised it yet. And Jesus was good. Jesus had changed the world through goodness, through being so wonderfully good. He had dutifully gone to Sunday School, and had enjoyed the stories of Jonah and the whale, and Daniel in the lion's den, but in his early teens he started to attend Bible Class. This was run by dear old Miss Ponder, who must have been all of seventy. Unmarried, she lived alone and had devoted her life to Jesus, though The Philanthropist did sometimes wonder if she had ever been kissed, or had the rather ponderous tits of Miss Ponder ever been fondled and squeezed when she was a pretty young thing in the Twenties. It was a preparatory class for Confirmation, for being received not only into the Church but into the body of Christ. The Philanthropist wanted to know what this meant, what would happen when he received the (representative, we weren't Catholics here) body of Christ in the guise of a wafer placed on his tongue. Miss Ponder told him that he would see the light. That all would become clear to him, that it would all make sense, that this would be the realisation of his life. To serve Jesus was the best thing a person could ever strive for. Really. And really he so wanted to discover how to become good.

The Philanthropist went along with it and knelt in line as the Bishop slowly placed the wafer on his tongue and held the silver chalice, the rim wiped with a neat white napkin, to his lips. He closed his eyes waiting for the revelation, for the light, for enlightenment, for the anointment from above, for the beginning of being good. Nothing. Absolutely nothing. No light, no descending dove, no inner knowledge at all. No redemption from his former sins. No new him. Nothing at all. Not even a glimmer of something. He opened his eyes and looked along the line at all his shut-eyed fellow confirmees, all kneeling on their scarlet velvet hassocks, and smiled inwardly. The game. This was another level of the game; that was all. They were all playing, and so he had played along too. Only *he* knew it was all a game, they actually believed – the fools. Later he asked Miss Ponder why the moment had been so underwhelming, why he had felt nothing. She explained that before true enlightenment you must have complete faith. "Surrender all doubt, have absolute faith and belief in Jesus, and all would be revealed," she assured him. Ah, so that's it; that's how the trick was accomplished.

London. He had visited London on a school trip to the National Gallery and loved the place. Not the Gallery with all those boring old paintings, but London itself. The noise, the rush, the sheer number of people all scurrying past, surely you could get lost easily in London. So lost that no-one would ever find you again. You could be anyone you wanted to be in London, anyone at all. Or no-one even, or lots of people, a different face for every place. Now, that *was* exciting. The possibilities were never-ending. You could disappear in London; you could live your life exactly on your own terms and be beholden to nobody. And this anonymity, this knowing but being unknown, unseen almost, became another obsession. And so, he made his plans in secret. The escape, that's what he called it. He would escape the life he was born into, the identity he had been given by others and become his own creation. Freedom at last. And so he planned his escape in the small hours in his tiny bedroom. Refining and defining his plans he never wrote anything down, it was all in his head. And he told no-one. There must be nothing to jeopardise his escape, and though brimming over with the excitement of it, he couldn't dare let anyone know. He told no-one, keeping his plan secret was almost as important as the idea itself.

He left one morning when no-one was watching. His father had gone to work and his mother was out early shopping. Ostensibly he was revising for his 'A' levels, studiously reading and making notes in his bedroom like the good son he was. His mother called up the stairs 'Bye, see you later', he grunted a reply and then he was alone. Well he was always alone, that went without saying, but now he was really alone. He watched out of their bedroom window as she bustled her large arse round the corner, her shopping trolley trundling behind her. He turned down the coverlet of their bed, leant in and smelt the sheets. Yes, that was her smell alright. This was the last time he would ever smell her, the last time he would see her pathetic face, the last time he would feel her trembling old lips graze his cheek, wiping the slimy trace of saliva away with the back of his hand as he hurried out of the door for school. He was trembling with the excitement of it all. This was the moment he had planned for so long, the escape was happening now. He neatly replaced the sheets, smoothed down the lacy counterpane and tidied up the net curtain at the window and quietly shut their bedroom door.

He closed his book and replaced it neatly on the shelf and reaching into his wardrobe pulled out the small suitcase he had packed the night before. He quietly closed the back door and walked down the same road his mother had walked only a few minutes earlier. He didn't look back once. He walked into the Building Society and withdrew the last twenty pounds in his savings account. The lady behind the counter asked him if he wanted the remaining six shillings and three pence, but no, he explained, he would be paying some money back in again soon, he wished to leave the account open thank you. He had drawn out over three hundred pounds during the preceding weeks, all in small amounts of twenty pounds or so, just as he had paid it all in from his monthly paper-round wages. His parents didn't know he had even opened the account, they had never asked him what he spent the paper-round money on.

He bought a cheap day return ticket to London, thinking that a single might arouse some suspicion. As the train pulled in he couldn't help letting out a quiet gasp of 'Yes', looking round quickly to make sure he had not been observed. As the train pulled out of the sleepy town he refused the temptation for one last look, he had seen it all before, and he knew that even though this was absolutely the last he would ever see of the place he wanted no memories to remain. A blank sheet, that was what he wanted this Suffolk life to become, no fond memories of a failed past. No memories at all. He was shedding that old skin and his new life was about to begin, that was all that mattered.

It was past six in the evening when his mother, tired of calling him down for his tea, went up to his bedroom and realised he wasn't there. Another three hours and he still hadn't come home. Where on earth could he be?

"Dad, do you think we should go to the Police Station?" she asked tremulously.

"No. What good would that do? He has left home. Face facts woman, some of his clothes are gone, and so has that suitcase we bought him last Christmas, and the tape recorder too."

"But I'm so worried Dad. Do you think he will be okay?" her teacup rattling with nerves as she steadied it into the saucer.

"Of course he will. Anyway he'll be back in a few days I 'spect. Soon as he discovers the world out there is a hard place, he'll be back. Tail between his legs too," and secretly furious with the boy he returned to his Daily Sketch. "Damned ungrateful I call it - after all we've done for the boy."

Whitechapel

He was up and out of his seat long before the train crept its weary way into Liverpool Street station, crawling past long stretches of black and lichen-covered Victorian brick walls that seemed to go on forever, the rails criss-crossing each other like some witches tangled hair, until at last the platform crept into view. Strangely he had no real idea where to go, months of planning his escape and no idea of where to go from here. He had been so meticulous in working out just when and how he would leave that he had given scant thought to what would happen when he actually got there. With a suitcase full of undaunted optimism and half a dozen shirts he was sure it would all work out, just get to London and his new life would start. Exactly where and how hadn't really occurred to him. He had over three hundred pounds in his pocket though, a fortune when you thought about it; he would be alright. The supreme confidence of youth filled him as suitcase in hand he walked across the vast and gloomy Victorian concourse, staring up at the filthy glass panels so high up they let in practically no daylight at all. He sought the 'Way Out' sign and freedom.

The sun was shining brightly as he strode out of the station and turned left, it could just as well have been right. A sunny day at last, it had rained for weeks back in Suffolk (was this a good omen). He turned his face and felt the healing warmth seep through his young body. No-one knew his name and no-one had any idea who he was at all. He was free. That was the beauty of his life at this precise moment; he was totally free. Unshackled by the accident of his birth, his parents, his school, his 'so-called friends' – all could be shaken off, forgotten, never to be thought of again. He would never return, he would never go back there, he was sure of that. Suffolk and all it had entailed, all of that claustrophobic small-mindedness was a thing of the past. He would put it all behind him, an unfortunate accident, best forgotten, if anyone asked he could make up his own history. He had read enough books; it shouldn't be that hard to imagine a different life for himself - and besides, who would ever know. Even his name, which he had had no part in choosing, could go; in fact he would ditch that stupid name altogether, he would never use it again. He would simply become another person; that should be no problem at all.

His heart had leaped when he had first heard his heroes 'The Beatles' singing 'She's Leaving Home'. That was exactly how he felt, and even though it was really a sad song (he ignored the mother finding the note that she left) he almost got a thrill just thinking about doing the same thing (and he didn't need the man from the motor-trade either, this was entirely his own doing). It was so easy – you left home and became a different person. No-one he had ever heard of had left home in Suffolk. Or not by simply walking out one morning and never coming back. One boy's father had disappeared; he had wandered off one day, but then had been found and was returned a week later, dazed and confused. Pathetic, he had returned to the same grindstone, nose ready to be positioned again. His life would continue the same as before he made his half-hearted break for freedom. That was not how this adventure would end; not at all. He would never be dragged back, apologetic and ashamed. This was for real. This was the start of his life and he was now in charge, not other people.

Whitechapel. Before he knew it he was in Whitechapel. A dingy run-down part of London full of newly arrived Asian sweatshops and old Victorian slum streets which he had never heard of, but actually it might just serve his purposes well. It was busy and grubby and no-one gave a second glance to this young man with his tiny suitcase looking bewildered all around him. Anonymity; that was the only thing he was looking for, anywhere he could be lost in would do. His worst fear, irrational though it might be, was that he might bump into someone who knew the old him. The possibility of being recognised before he could even assume his new identity haunted him, but of course nobody did. Nobody noticed him at all. He was just another run-away; they'd seen plenty of those in the past, and nothing to get excited about.

But practicalities forced themselves in on his moment of glory; somewhere to stay for the night, that was his first priority and something to eat of course, he hadn't eaten since breakfast over six hours ago. He had never had to feed himself before; his devoted mother always had three meals a day ready for him. No mother to look after him now though, now he would have to buy his own food, and lodgings too. Looking around he spotted a hand-written sign in the window of a six story dark Edwardian brick building, "Evening meal and Bed, 19/6." That didn't seem too bad. He pushed open the heavy wooden door and walked in. It was filthy. And dark too, lit by a single un-shaded and fly-speckled yellowing bulb. And it stunk too; cabbage and piss in almost equal quantities.

"Well, what you want, young man?" an old woman in a grubby pinny snapped at him, as she came up from a dark staircase leading down into some subterranean lower levels.

"I saw the sign and wondered about a room for the night." He replied far too politely.

"Done a runner?" the old woman took the fag out of her mouth and pointed at his suitcase with it.

"Not exactly" he replied, somewhat defensively.

"Makes no odds to me luv. Come on, follow me."

And up the six flights of stairs he hauled his rather heavy suitcase, with the reel to reel carefully wrapped in his best pullover and a handful of clothes jammed in the sides to stop it sliding about, and though devastated at the 'room' she showed him he decided it would be far too much trouble to refuse and try to find somewhere else that evening. The room was almost empty, except for a threadbare rug covering half the wooden floorboards and three iron-railing beds with filthy mattresses, one in each corner and a rickety old table in the other.

"That's your bed over there. Blankets in that cupboard." (cigarette pointing to a door in the corner) "Money up front now or you're out on your ear. Dinner downstairs in an hour. Okay?"

He hesitated to ask about the occupants of the other beds but she caught his wary glance straight away. "They'll be back later. Out begging I expect, if they 'asn't pissed it all away by now." And as her laugh broke into a rackety cough she shook her head-scarfed head and said "Don't worry they won't bite. Might smell a bit, but that don't matter none. You won't find nowhere cheaper nowhere - I can tell you that."

"No, this will do nicely, thank you." He smiled politely. But inside he felt like crying, this was not how he had envisaged his new life beginning. One night he kept telling himself, just one night then I'll find somewhere decent to live. He just had to put up with this squalor for one night.

"Toilet and sink on the second floor, knock before you try the handle, there's no lock on the inside." He was about to ask why not but she beat him to it. "Don't want no-one locking theirself's inside and toppin' themselfs do we deary? Bad for business." And she cackled and coughed all the way downstairs leaving our rather bewildered Philanthropist to survey his newfound kingdom. One night he kept repeating to himself, one night.

The two tramps who returned soon after he had eaten a rather stodgy suet pudding and two veg. alone in the 'dining room' turned out to be quite harmless, but she was right, they did smell pretty dreadful. Tired old men who existed on handouts and a bit of charity, spending any spare money on booze. They may actually have only been in their forties but they looked much older, and shabby and worn-out, weary from living on the streets. It must be a hard life, he thought, but maybe they were happy in their own way. At least no-one was telling them what to do all day, but that wasn't the life for him at all. He was going to be somebody, just you wait and see. They talked far too much and far too long, muttering to each other or maybe just to themselves, and he had real trouble in falling asleep in a room with other people. He had always had his own bedroom, his private sanctuary, to himself. For as long as he could remember his mother had knocked before turning the handle and letting herself in, apologising for disturbing him. Politeness had been everything in their home; raised voices never disturbed the air, angry thoughts were stifled, peace had reigned. Just for one night, that's all.

Worst of all he could smell them right across the room, crusty body odour and cheap booze, and they farted and snored all night too, but he must have dropped off eventually. When he woke they were both gone and the sun was streaming through the torn curtains slung across the grimy window. He quickly reached under the bed, but his suitcase and stuff were all there, and the wallet with his precious money was safe under the very itchy pillowcase-less pillow.

He dressed quickly, desperate to escape the house. His first priority was to find somewhere to live, and pretty quick. He asked the old woman what was the best way to find a permanent room.

"Evenin' News. Comes out round lunchtime, you can buy it everywhere, only tuppence." She said, the fag bobbing up and down as she spoke. "Aren't you staying here tonight son? I thought you liked it here." Coughing and laughing at the same time.

He smiled sweetly "Best place in town I should say, but unfortunately I shall have to disappoint you. But thanks for the kind offer." And she laughed even longer, until the coughing took her over completely and she reached into her pinny for another fag.

He scoured the ads for rooms to let in the paper and eventually finding an un-vandalised phone box he rung the number and before the day was out had moved in. It was it must be said the cheapest room he could find in the whole three columns – two pounds a week; preserving his small hoard of savings seemed the wisest thing to do. He would have to get a job soon, and again he had no idea how to. They didn't give you a manual at school about how these things were done. He suspected he would need papers, and that would mean some sort of contact with the school he had just run way from, if not his parents. He had never seen or asked to see his birth certificate but suspected he might need it, or some form of identification. But he was no longer that person, he was a new man now, he hated the idea of using that name ever again. He was sure he had heard people talk about cards. When you lost your job people said they had given you your cards, didn't they? What were cards? How did you get them? Why hadn't he thought things through thoroughly?

The room itself was tiny, but at least it was clean. There was no space left unused, a single bed, a tiny wardrobe, a small chest of drawers that could only be used when the wardrobe door was shut, a single Belling electric hob and a sink, and all for just two pounds a week. It wasn't much but it was a start, he was here in his own place, his real life was about to start.

Stoke Newington

He was in Stoke Newington, North London – he had never heard of the place before. It was, like Whitechapel and most of East London, pretty run-down; red-brick thirties blocks of council flats with washing strung along the balconies, and crumbling Victorian houses full of black and brown families, half-boarded up shops and pubs on every corner. But he was safe. That was the most important thing. Day two and he had escaped and buried himself so deep that no-one, no parents, no school, could ever find him. No-one would be able to drag him back – he was free at last; his new life just waiting for him.

He would have to find a job soon and that might prove difficult. His money wouldn't last forever. He was sure you needed identification of some sort, and the last thing he wanted was to tell his potential employers his real name. They would be sure to ask him about his parents and school, probably insisting on contacting them. He never wanted to see either of them again, school or his parents. He had made the break. In fact he had made the break years ago, the sentimental link had been broken years before the physical. He had come to London to disappear, to re-invent himself. He would never go back, never return. Dylan had sung, 'Don't think twice, It's alright.' Dylan had left home and bummed his way to New York;

when he sang in the folk clubs surely no-one had asked him for his papers. But this was London and not New York, and besides our Philanthropist was no folk-singing troubadour, but that's how he wanted to live his life; no ties, especially with the past, just living for the present. In fact, just living – that would do for starters.

The last thing he wanted was to get trapped again. And yet that was exactly what he did do. Stupid, yes, but love is blind (and stupid). Love, that overwhelming emotion he had rejected stole up on him and before he knew the net was slipped over his shoulders and he was caught. The Beatles had sung about Love, but that was just for the girls, to get them into bed; everyone secretly understood that. Didn't they? He knew that Love was for fools but somehow he couldn't stop himself. If it were as simple as that he wouldn't have got trapped, it's just that sometimes you can't see the trap closing over you. You think you have discovered freedom, a warm safe blanket, but then when it's too late you find out it was just another net to catch you in.

He saw her in the pool. He had decided to go for a swim. He had always enjoyed swimming. It was like another world, floating, head laid back, the water just lapping his ears and drifting effortlessly on his back with just the gentlest of kicks now and then to stop himself from sinking beneath the water. The way the water glides over your body as you carve into it, your front crawl a knife slicing up the heavy water was exquisite. Or that moment you dive from a board and go from one medium into another, the warm thin air then the icy-cold semi-fluid water; that exquisite moment of transition, the whoosh in your ears, the sudden deceleration as you instinctively stop falling and rise to the surface. In Suffolk they had an open-air pool, nothing between you, the water and the sky. He loved that feeling – you could be anywhere at all lying on your back staring up at the sun and the clouds and oh-so-blue sky. Another less permanent escape maybe.

But the pool here in Stoke Newington was a crumbling red-brick indoor pool. Old cracking concrete painted blue and cream, enclosed, shut-in and far too noisy with the shrieks of kids and stinking of chlorine too. The ceiling felt too low, even when he closed his eyes he couldn't shut out the noise bouncing off the too-low ceiling. He wasn't really enjoying the experience but he had been bored and thought that swimming might fill in an hour or so of time. He was avoiding the grim reality of finding a job, escaping again. But it hadn't worked, he realised it had been a mistake, the dream-like state he was seeking would never work here. About to give in and return to the changing rooms he saw her swimming around the shallow end. There was something different about her. He couldn't tell exactly what it was, her blonde hair wasn't even wet from her careful swimming, she was slightly chubby, and kept blinking, looking all around her as if she was lost. Short-sightedness he would later discover, but this vulnerability, this spatial unawareness made her seem lonely, made her seem somehow in need of him, or so he thought. He had this overwhelming feeling; he knew he had to talk to her. And this from the boy who had studiously avoided talking to the girls he had become obsessed with; the last thing he wanted was to speak to them, to break the spell. But she was different, this one. And so was he of course; no longer the shy one, afraid of speaking to girls, content to dream and wank about them, but never letting them exist as real people. And a new person might be brave enough to chat her up, something the old him was hopeless at. And there was something about her, something that drew him to her. He could never explain it, even to himself, what it was that had crept under his defences. Love; that was what it must have been - it was the only explanation. But that was for later, when he tried to make sense of it all, for now he just knew he had to talk to her.

He had been in London nearly a week and hadn't really talked to anyone; a brief conversation with his landlady, a few exchanged words at the fish and chip shop or the grubby local newsagents. He still hadn't done anything about finding a job, he would need to go to a library and find out what papers he would need but this was Saturday and the library was closed. Besides he had the cushion of his savings, no need to worry just yet. He had come to London to begin living, not to worry about minor things like getting a job. He put it to the back of his mind, a problem for another day. He knew immediately he had to speak to this girl, and though he had always been shy of 'chatting girls up', had got to know them first at school or at the youth club and even then he had let them do the talking first, he somehow plucked up the courage. Or the new person he now was did, and so what if she laughed at him, as he had always dreaded back in Suffolk, he could just smile and walk away. London was big enough to lose himself in; he need never see her again.

Some sort of recklessness overtook him, what had he got to lose. And besides he was someone new here in London, not that shy loner he used to be. He swam closer and closer and she noticing him, kept swimming away, but like a shark he circled his prey, swimming closer and fixing her with a stare. There was a slight air of panic in the air, was she scared or excited by his attention. Neither of them was sure and so the game played itself out. She half-splashed him away, but he just laughed and said "What's your name?"

"Haven't got one." She automatically replied, knowing this would just encourage him, but it was the first thing that came into her mind.

"Hello little Miss Haven'tGotOne. Is that really your name?"

"Look, just get lost okay." She was a bit worried now, it wasn't that she didn't like him; it was his persistence that slightly perturbed her. Besides without her glasses she couldn't really see him. Not clearly enough anyway.

"But I can't. I am lost already. I have no idea where I am or indeed who I am. Your beauty has entranced me." Where had all this come from? He spoke the words but didn't recognise thinking them first; it was as if someone, something else, had taken him over. He had been a thinker; he was cautious and rehearsed his words before speaking. Until now that is.

She laughed and swam away. He swam after her. Reluctantly she agreed to meet him outside the pool. Maybe to get rid of him, maybe to play for time, she wasn't really sure. He climbed out of the water and got changed quickly and waited for her. And waited. And waited. She eventually came out. She had her glasses on now, her extra protection from the world, and looking round, she saw him sitting on the wall and walked the other way. Ah, so that's how she wants to play the game. He caught up with her. The sun was shining, the world looked wonderful. She was wonderful, life was good after all.

"Hello again" he said looking straight at her eyes; even her glasses couldn't protect her now.

"Oh, it's you. I thought you wouldn't be here." She dissembled.

"That's not true. You knew I would be, that's why you looked for me, and then walked the other way. Don't you like me?" The new him spoke with a new authority, a cavalier directness he didn't recognise.

"I dunno know. Yet. I might do. Depends." Childish answers but she was little more than a child and new at this game.

"Okay. Let me walk with you awhile." And he was suddenly her friend. They walked and walked, up and down streets and in and out of Clissold Park, and all the time he talked. He couldn't remember about what at all, but talk he did. And his talking somehow reassured her and slowly she accepted him. He made her laugh, he made her smile and there hadn't been much to smile about so far in her life. He was funny, he was different from the boys at school and he made her feel good inside.

And that was how it started. Was it boredom, was it a random choice or was it a deeper attraction, another obsession or something different? He didn't know, he just knew that when he was with her he was elated. He was someone else entirely, he was ecstatically happy. And he was completely unaware as the net was gently draped around both his and her shoulders. It felt quite snug, this feeling of happiness and security he hadn't really felt before and actually incredibly quickly he found that he had fallen deeply in love with this girl.

He took her to the pictures and they kissed. He had kissed girls before but never like this. He was trembling as he kissed her, it started way down in the pit of his stomach, or even further down than that. He was lost in this kissing, it was as if the kissing was taking him over. And slowly they progressed until one evening on his narrow bed-sit bed they made love. It was the first time for both of them, and it was alright because they loved each other. They were each giving themselves to the other, unified in this act of togetherness. In his imagination he likened them to John and Yoko, two virgins indeed. This was true love. He had never experienced anything like this. He had totally lost control, and he the one who had wanted to control everything. But for the first time in his life it really didn't matter. Being with her was all that mattered. He was lost when he was with her and lost without her. He couldn't stop thinking about her, the way she looked up at him, blinking nervously. The way her hair fell over her eyes, and the way she tossed her head, the way she walked, the way she talked. Everything about her dragged him deeper and deeper in love with her. Every moment spent apart he was thinking about her when he should have been thinking about getting a job.

The Philanthropist

He spent his money, his precious hoard, on her. Meals in Wimpy bars, visits to the West End to see the new film releases, little presents for her, nights just sitting and talking or walking round and round the streets of Stoke Newington, hand in hand, two star-crossed lovers – it soon went and suddenly he was down to about fifty pounds and realised he had to sort himself out. Get a job, anything would do, he just needed to be earning some money somehow.

This was about the same time as she told him she was pregnant. Of course they had both been so much in love, blindly in love, that they hadn't given a thought to contraception. It hadn't even crossed his mind; he had been so besotted by her beauty, by the joy of being completely and utterly lost in the moment that the most basic biological consequence of their actions had escaped him. And she too had simply gone along with this first love of hers, unquestioningly following his lead and now she was scared. She suddenly felt all alone in the world and she was frightened and started sobbing as the words spilled out of her. She was crying as she told him, scared perhaps that he would abandon her, that she would be on her own again. She knew he had run away once, maybe he would run away from her too. And he was everything to her, she loved him so much.

Suddenly his world collapsed, or the pretty world he had constructed, (eternal love and all that) collapsed. Like a balloon suddenly deflated his ever expanding unlimited world had rapidly shrunk to these four walls, this sobbing girl and the consequences of his thoughtlessness. He had never thought she might get pregnant. He hadn't been thinking at all. She was still a child, only fifteen (though he hadn't known that when he first met her, not that it had stopped him, of course) and he not much older and like children they hadn't thought about the consequences. They had drifted into love, drifted into kissing, drifted into sex itself. They were so besotted with each other that they hadn't even considered what would happen if she got pregnant.

"How far gone are you?" he asked.

"I am not sure, about eight weeks I think. I have missed one period anyway, and my next should be due any day now, but I don't think it's going to happen. I know it isn't. I know I am pregnant." She blinked up at him.

"Oh God, what are we going to do?" his head held despairingly in his hands.

"I can't tell my Mum and Dad. They'll kill me, throw me out. I know they will. I don't know what to do. I'm so scared. I really am so frightened. Take me away from here, please. I can't face my Mum and Dad. Please." And she looked so pathetic, so vulnerable he wanted to, he needed to be strong for her.

"Don't worry – I'll look after you." And he put his arms around her and held her. But was he holding her or holding onto her? Holding her up or holding her down? Was he her saviour or she his life belt? For a while they just sat on the edge of the bed in his tiny bedsit rocking slowly back and forth, as he patted her hair and whispered "I love you" over and over again into her tiny shell-like ears. He was as lost as she was, the only thought he had was to comfort her, to wipe away those tears; if only he could wipe away the baby as easily. And for a few minutes it was enough. They loved each other; it was just them against the whole world. They loved each other and it was enough. And then it came to him …

And the solution was simple. Run away. They could run away and become new people. He had run away before, just a couple of short months ago and the sky hadn't fallen in (if only he had looked up). We could run away together. To Scotland. You could get married there at sixteen, (or so he had heard) without your parent's permission. Running away was easy. After all, all you had to do was buy the ticket. "Don't worry – I'll look after you."

Edinburgh

He bought the tickets. Two singles to Edinburgh for the following day. It was a night bus leaving Waterloo at seven in the evening and arriving at five the next day. She met him at the local tube station after school, lugging the suitcase he had given her, full of her clothes, behind her. They barely spoke all the way to Waterloo; what was there to say? They were both shell-shocked, war-weary despite their tender years – all they wanted was to escape. There was no heating on the bus so she huddled close into him all the way, burying her head in the warmth of his jacket, his coat draped over the two of them. He stared out of the window the whole journey as the lights from small towns came and went. Sometimes he was looking out into pure darkness. All he could see out of the window was pitch black night and the raindrops as they skidded across the glass. Darkness everywhere and it was raining and cold. Another wet and windy November, why did it rain so much in England? He kept wiping the condensation bloom from the window with the side of his hand and he still couldn't see anything out there but utter darkness. Was this what his new life, his famous new beginning, had come to - a never-ending darkness? He hugged her ever tighter – she was all he had. His dwindling savings were almost gone, and here he was running away again. He was becoming aware at long last that he was trapped again. He had run away to escape the trap of a conventional life, of falling for the old tricks. And now here he was a victim of the unkindest trick of all, he was well and truly trapped this time. But still he loved her; unconditionally, blindly, ferociously certain of his love. He would defend that love against anyone, but it was a trap all the same, maybe the oldest one of all. For three months he had been living in some sort of dreamtime, wasting his days and putting off the prospect of getting a job; he hadn't been thinking at all. All he had existed for, every waking moment was waiting to see her again, to hold her, to be held, to be with her was all that mattered. And now she was with him alright. There was no escaping the sleeping entity beside him now, even had he dared let himself imagine such a thing.

She slept the whole long journey, but he was wide awake. Maybe more awake now than he had been for months. He was tired too but nothing would let him close his eyes, he stared out all night and all he saw was darkness out there. The bus slowly pulled into the bus garage at Edinburgh. They were almost the only passengers left as he shook her gently awake. The dawn was a couple of hours away yet. It was still raining; a soft but persistent drizzle that felt like gentle spray on your face but soaked through your clothes, right to the bone. Welcome to Edinburgh, the torn poster flapping in the rain declared. Yeah, well. He hauled their case out of the rack and down the stairs. They were the last off the bus; she had taken ages waking up. He had left the tape recorder and most of his clothes behind, the suitcase his parents had once bought him was now filled with her clothes and just a few of his.

They walked slowly up a steep hill towards Leith and saw a sign for vacant rooms. He paid the five pounds the landlady demanded for the week before even seeing the room. It was a narrow tenement building, grey granite, dark and foreboding, six or seven floors tall with a wide staircase and rooms to the left and right on every landing. Their room was near the top. He would always remember the wide stone steps worn to a dip in the middle of each step by thousands of shoes. How many desperate hopeless couples had trudged up them hauling their entire worldly possessions in cases just like his he wondered? And how many had ended up happy? Too late to worry about that now. They shut the door and the world behind them and fell exhausted onto the bed. Bright red nylon sheets, but what the fuck. They had made it. He slept for a while and she was still curled up and huddled in his arms. He woke, restlessly looked at his watch, kissed her and went out to get some food and a newspaper. He saw an advert in a sweetshop window "Bar staff wanted - no experience needed." He asked someone the way; it was only two streets away, he quickly walked there. He gave a false name, another one. This was beginning to become a habit by now. The one she knew him by was false too; after all he would never have had the nerve to talk to her if he still had his old name. The guy behind the bar didn't ask for papers or anything except could he start that night, he was desperate, people kept letting him down. His job would be collecting and washing glasses mostly. A pound a night, cash in hand. Did he want the job? Yes, he would be there at six.

He returned with some sort of hope and self-belief in his heart. It wasn't going to be so bad. He had found a job and no papers needed; they would soon find a proper room, maybe a flat even. They would get married as soon as she was sixteen. She would have the baby. They had each other. It was going to be alright.

Before he could tell her about the job she broke her news to him.

"I've rung my mother. I used the phone in the hallway downstairs." She explained, blinking up at him.

"What did you do that for? You didn't tell her where we are did you?" he cautioned, thoughts of Police and arrest crowding his mind.

"Yes. She said to come home, it would be alright. She'll sort everything out." She was so relieved, she couldn't help but smile.

"And what did you say to that? You don't imagine they'll let you have the baby, do you? They will stop us from seeing each other, you know that don't you?"

"No they won't. Nothing will keep us apart. We love each other. But I can't have this baby. I never wanted to have a baby, I'm far too young. My Mum says she'll arrange an abortion. She says it's all going to be alright. I want to … I have to go home. I can't do this. You do see that don't you. Please. Let's go home. I need to go home. Please." And as the tears welled up in those little eyes and she took off her glasses and rubbed them with the backs of her tiny hands he knew he had lost. Even if it hadn't been much of a winning game he knew he had lost.

And it was all over, their little Scottish adventure, their great escape. Here he was, our hero, returning on the night bus, blinking back his own tears. Scared, really scared now of what awaited them back in London. She was sleeping, huddled into his jacket with his coat draped over them both. He was staring out into the cold wet night as the lights from small towns they passed through gave way to utter and complete darkness.

Waterloo

He put her into a taxi, stuffed the suitcase beside her, shoved his last fiver into the driver's hand and gave him the address. He leaned in and told her he couldn't face her parents, the police, whatever. He would be in touch, he promised. He was looking at the suitcase, not at her. She just blinked back her incomprehension at him. Oh, those eyes nearly did for him again. He had rehearsed the lines on the journey back, but he couldn't look into her eyes as he said the words. He didn't want to see those tearful trusting eyes of hers; he knew he might not be strong enough. And he needed to be strong to lose her, to let her go. She looked shocked and as the taxi pulled slowly away she stared at him out of the back window; in disbelief or relief he could never quite work out. Maybe it was just that short-sighted blinking stare, trying to make him out in the dark morning; that same myopic stare he had fallen for in the first place. One part of him wanted to run after the taxi, to stop it and throw himself in beside her, but he stood rooted to the spot in some sort of self-loathing determination. He turned away before the taxi disappeared and slouched off towards the river, utterly heartbroken. He was devastated by what he had just done and was completely lost. Lost for words to describe how he felt. He had just waved away the one thing he loved. He had deserted her, abandoned her to the tender mercies of her mother, the authorities, facing the abortion alone; he had left her on her own. But he was out here in the bitter cold and on his own too.

He had killed the very thing he had loved the most. The only thing he had ever loved in fact. A terrible price to pay for his mistakes, but he knew if he stayed with her the mistakes would simply carry on. They hadn't stood a chance, he could see that now. She had been far too young and he too selfish. He should have gotten a job, taken things slower - used a 'French Letter' for Christ's sake. No, they had never stood a chance; he was like poison, and he had infected them both with his venomous love. They would drag each other down, each clinging like seaweed to the other's neck and down and down they would fall. And sooner or later he would have to untangle himself and escape. Sooner or later, and rather than drown later he had to escape now. To save himself - and her too, at least he had saved her from him and his pernicious touch. Even though this felt worse than drowning, worse than death itself – he knew he had to do it. Better now than later with a baby and all. It wasn't her fault at all, but his. He had pursued her, he had stolen her childhood - he had wanted her, he had charmed her, he had seduced her and he had taken her. He had thoughtlessly got her pregnant and now he had deserted her. His self-loathing was complete. His only consolation, if that was what you could call it, was that through it all he had loved her. He was sure of that. He had truly loved her. Misguided love, selfish and reckless love maybe, but love none the less. He looked back over the last few months and couldn't quite believe how things had turned out. Four months ago he was safe in Suffolk; nice home, nice school, a popular boy, friends and family around him. Safe. Safe, but trapped. He had felt trapped by it all, by that closeness, that security, that unconditional love of his parents – he was determined not to play their game. Any of them – they were all playing the same game, he couldn't live his life like that. He had decided to escape, but had fallen back into another and deeper trap at the first opportunity. He had been free for just a few short days when anything had been possible. He should have buckled down, got a job and started earning some money. He wasn't scared of work; he had got up even on the coldest wintry mornings and done his paper round. But he had fallen into some sort of daydream, and looking back it was all a dream, running away, that awful room in Whitechapel, the swimming pool, meeting her and even the desperate flight to and humble return from Edinburgh too. Just a dream he was having that had somehow turned into a nightmare. He had woken up in the nick of time.

He had been okay, the worst was surely over. He had escaped and no-one had found him, no-one had come to fetch him back. Four months he had eluded them, he must be safe by now. And then all this had happened. Falling in love; tumbling blindly stupidly but elatedly in love. Sex, love, call it what you will, but he had felt it. He had really felt it. It had taken him over so completely. He had never felt like that before, and he wasn't sure if he ever would again. Or more to the point if he would ever let himself become that lost again. That trapped. It had been another trap, hadn't it? Love was just another trap. That was how the game was played and how so many lost. He had almost lost the game; he had almost lost himself too. He had certainly lost all his money. He was broke. No home, not even a room. He thought about returning to his little room in Stoke Newington, to retrieve the tape machine and his few possessions, he still had the key. But what if the Police had been to his digs? He couldn't be doing with the Police. Her parents would surely have called the Cops. They would find out about his name, who he really had been, not the name she had known him by, not the person she had fallen in love with at all. Maybe his parents would come to London for him. Maybe he would be forced to return. Head hung in shame and everyone, teachers, school-friends, relatives; they would all know. No, he couldn't bear the shame of it, and he knew if he was defeated in that way he might never have the courage to escape again. Better to walk away from all of that. He still had his anonymity; no-one knew who he was or where he was. He was leaning over the balustrade and watching the murky ink-black waters of the Thames. He threw the key in the water. A few small coins were all he now possessed, but he would be alright, no-one would find him here. London was big enough to be completely lost in forever.

And lost he became. Truly lost. So lost he wasn't sure he would ever find himself again. He drifted onto the streets, sleeping in doorways and begging for coins outside theatres and tube stations. Doing odd jobs for cash when he could and sleeping rough on sheets of cardboard, then an old sleeping bag he bought off another tramp. He grew a thick black beard, his hair hung long down his back, matted and dirty, he looked ten years older. And the only thing he had to console himself with was that no-one knew who he was, no-one knew anything about him at all. He had lost everything but gained anonymity, no-one would ever find him here on the streets of London and no-one would ever know who he really was.

He only meant it to last a few days. He would somehow get a job, there must be people who would pay you in cash; he would get back on his feet again soon. But as the days stretched slowly into weeks he realised he could actually survive like this. He was cold and dirty, often hungry - but he was still alive, he was sure of that. And no-one could find him; they would never find him now. He had escaped the trap; at the last moment he had heard the catch release and the unwinding spring was bringing the metal bar hurtling right down on his head. He had swerved and it had missed him; he was free.

Two years passed, two freezing winters trying to keep body and soul together when food was scarce, warmth scarcer and a touch of human kindness impossible to find. And through the rain and snow he hugged himself for warmth, shivering and wearing all his clothes, all the cast-offs he scavenged, layer upon layer and still feeling the cold piercing through, but consoling himself that this wouldn't last forever. He just needed a break - a chance was all he needed. Two summers when he would lay on the grass in Hyde Park enjoying the warm touch of the sun until night came and he would slouch back to the shabby streets around Waterloo. The ugly sixties concrete warren, the subways, the low-ceilinged maze of walkways became his night-time lair, here where the dregs of society congregated, the hopeless losers, the persistent drunks and the barely alive. But at least in the sun lying on the grass he was as free as anyone else. Nobody paid any attention to him, here in Hyde Park, staring up at the clouds and begging the sun to come out from behind those dark clouds once again. At least they didn't charge you for the warmth of the sun; that was free. And he was free too, free to walk any streets he wanted, free to piss up against any wall in the night-time, free to think about how he might really begin again next time.

What was it, this freedom he craved? He knew that he was different; he had always thought he was far more intelligent than everyone else and yet here he was wasting two years, desperately clinging on to some idea of independence and anonymity. Cold at night, dirty and hungry most days – was all of this worth it, just to not have to conform, to not be part of the very society he despised. Apparently so, because he was on the streets for two hard years; or maybe he was just making plans, daydreams that one day he might eventually realise. There were times he wanted to give up, but where do you go when you are on the street? There is no place any lower; even the Police would give him short shrift. He knew he would get out of this depressing cycle one day, he just wasn't sure how. And besides once you got over the first few weeks, the first cold winter, once you found you could survive that, and then the summers weren't so bad, you could lay in the park all day and sleep away your worries. Somehow there was always a way to get a few pennies for some food, an occasional job washing dishes until they kicked you out, a new doorway to sleep in. London was a never-ending series of doorways;

just none were opening for him. And then it became a life. People are so adaptable they will accept any suffering, any deprivation, as long as they are still alive.

There were plenty of others, tramps, down and outs, call them what you will; mostly older but a few runaways his age or even younger. He didn't really talk to them, they weren't like him. They were no-hopers; they were piss-artists or even worse - druggies. He avoided them and they in turn avoided him. It was as if they knew instinctively he wasn't one of them. And he knew for sure he wasn't one of them either. They would sit around a fire of old pallets or cardboard in the winter sharing a bottle or a packet of fags, reciting the same old stories of their day - but he shied away from them, he didn't share anything, he kept himself to himself. As the firelight flickered and the smoke passed over him, he burrowed deeper into his rancid sleeping bag and tried to think about his life. Alcohol scared him and he had tried smoking at school behind the bike shed, and coughed so badly he never did it again. A rite of passage like so many others he was almost proud of failing. Maybe he was scared of all addictions, or was it just the terrible effect it had on so many of the rough sleepers he saw. He knew he had to stay away from booze. It was one of the hardest traps to ever get out of, he knew that much.

He had nothing in common with these drinkers, these hopeless failures. They even saw themselves as failures, whereas The Philanthropist knew that whatever anyone else saw on the outside, the beard, the ragged clothes, the split shoes, inside he was no failure. He just hadn't really got started yet, he was still formulating his plans. It took him a long time to get over the loss of his first love, the death of the dream, the end of that love; of all love perhaps. He dreamed about her most nights, the softness of her skin, the way her hair would slip down over her eyes, the way she looked up at him, her eyes widening as they adjusted to the light. And being next to her, sleeping beside her, being wrapped in her loving arms and held so close; he missed her smile, her eyes, all of her, and when she woke after sleep, all bleary-eyed and yawning. He missed that feeling of lying safe in her arms, harboured against the roughness of the world. But even that very safety had ended up being a trap. Maybe all love, all close friendship, was a trap. Maybe if he was to succeed he would need to cut out that emotional weakness, to harden his heart against love itself. So he shared nothing, kept himself isolated, insulated, mumbling to himself and he talked to no-one unless he had to. Some days he would speak to no other person at all, shuffling along the streets of London, head down, deep in thought, and talking to no-one. But he did talk to the sad-eyed middle-aged woman who ran the soup-kitchen on Friday nights or rather she insisted on talking to him. She refused to take his silence for an answer and persisted.

"Why don't you sort yourself out, sonny? I see you here week after week, and you're not like most of them. I never smell the drink on you, and you're still quite young. In your early twenties I'd say." Cocking her head to one side he saw she was taking the measure of him.

"Yeah, well. I never liked alcohol, and I don't smoke or do drugs either." He said defensively.

"So, what's stopping you from getting a life? You can't be doing this for a career now. You have got to grow up sometime." And she smiled at him, the first person in weeks he had a smile from.

"I suppose so - I just need a break I suppose." He mumbled, eager to get away.

"Listen. I know some people in Camden Town. They run a sort of charity centre, a rehabilitation place. They try and get young people off the streets and back into normal life." She tried to engage him, even though he was half turning away from her.

"I'm not sure I want to get back into what you call normal life." And for the first time he looked at and not past her. She was kind, and that was something he hadn't known in a long time.

"Don't be so daft. You can make life what you want, you know. You don't have to live by all of the rules. As long as you appear to be obeying most of them, that's all that really matters." She looked down at her hands, turning them over and back, and then back at him. "Most of us live a secret life; none of my so-called friends know I do this."

"Then why do you? Do this, I mean. It can't be much fun." For the first time in years he was talking to someone, and he was struggling with the unfamiliarity of it.

"I do it because I want to. I have my reasons. I wasn't always a 'good' person. I have done lots of things I am ashamed of in my time." She was looking down, her mousy brown hair cascading gently over her face; she brushed it aside with ring-less hands, tucking the bangs behind her ears. "Maybe this is my way of paying life back. Who knows?" and she shrugged her shoulders. "Anyway all I am saying is I can help you, but only if you want to be helped. Think about it. I'm here every Friday, just let me know."

Camden Town

And Joan did help him. Joan - that was her name, or the name she gave him. And Keith was the name he gave her. Keith, because of Keith Richards of the Stones. He liked the sound of the name. It seemed to suit him somehow, so for a few years he became Keith. Keith James. Keep it short, easy to remember and easy to forget when the time would come for forgetting. He moved into her small flat in Camden Town. There was never any question of him staying in one of the shelters; Joan made it clear she was going to look after him. Her flat was tiny, just the one bedroom. Keith slept on the pull-out sofa at first, but they both knew he would soon be sharing her bed.

She was nearly thirty years older than he, but in a strange way it never bothered him. Her skin was remarkably soft, where he imagined it might have lost some of that suppleness of youth. He sunk into her arms and the warm roundness of her ample breasts, her soft body wrapping itself around him, enveloping him in a cloud of comfort. It felt like coming home, coming in out of the cold and he had been out in the cold for a long time. This was the first human touch in two years. It was only sex, he told himself. He was careful not to fall in love with her, not to be trapped again, though he had to admit that even if it was only sex it was pretty damn good. His first love had been a virgin like him, but Joan was experienced.

She knew a lot more about the human body and what turned men on too. He sometimes wondered about the past she carefully avoided talking about. She hadn't always led a good life she had said; maybe she had been some sort of prostitute in her younger days, or a stripper. He was still naive about these things and thought the two might be one and the same. She later admitted that she had indeed been on the game a couple of times in her thirties; she had acquired a nasty cocaine habit and had found that selling sex was the easiest way to pay for it. She was clean now and mostly did charity work; and no, she wasn't ashamed of what she had done but it was in the past, as was her habit; and no, she had no desire to return to either.

"End of story" she said, putting her finger to his lips to stop his further enquires as she kissed her way down his body (why are men so fascinated by a woman's former lovers). And she was totally uninhibited when it came to sex; nothing shocked her, though actually Keith was. Shocked at first, but soon enjoying this liberated feeling that anything was okay. Whatever she might have done when she wasn't living this good life didn't bother him, even the drugs – as long as he wasn't dragged into another trap. As long as he didn't love her, as long as he could keep it like this, just sex. Falling in love again, getting trapped, that was his biggest fear.

She trimmed his hair, cut and shaped his beard for him and took him to the Sanctuary Centre, a small charity trying to get people off the streets and back into what some might call real life. They never asked him for papers or any sort of proof of who he was, or why he had ended up on the street. They were interested only in his future, not his past, or so they said. He was reluctant at first but they were patient, they had met a lot of resistance before. They suggested a couple of local restaurants where he could get casual work washing-up in the kitchens, no questions asked and no papers needed. He tried it but only lasted three days, the heat, the constant pile of dishes and saucepans, the abusive shouting of the chefs were all too much for him. He wasn't sure he would be able to work for anyone at all, it was too much like being at school, and school was all he had known. Someone suggested he try working on the market.

Camden market in the early seventies was a mix of a traditional market, cheap household goods, one or two fruit and veg stalls and a few hippy-style people selling candles and herbal remedies and second hand clothes. He started working for cash on one of the stalls and soon learned the ropes. It sold second hand books and records. This was something he understood, he knew all about books and records and he loved it. If he had no customers he was busy sorting the albums out, or reading one of the books. Being out in all weathers hardly bothered him, and the punters preferred silence to conversation anyway. But when he was asked about the records he knew stuff; producers and engineers, the band members and other records they had made and so people started to come to him for advice. They also brought him records to sell; they trusted that he would give them a fair price. He had a sort of honesty about him, with his longish hair and newly-trimmed beard he looked like one of them, not a trader. Before long he had taken over the stall while the owner moved into vintage clothes. Keith bought the entire stock for twenty pounds, paid for at a pound a week. And the stall soon paid for itself. He bought cheap, only giving fifty pence or less to the constant stream of young men wanting ready cash for sixties albums and selling them on for pounds. He seemed to know by instinct what would sell, which bands might be popular, and which to reject. Books and records interested him and therefore he thrived. Soon he had a roaring business stretching over three stalls and he was becoming a destination, especially at the weekends.

"So, this is by the Beatles? I thought I had all their records." Someone asked him one day.

"That's a bootleg, not an official release. A sound engineer probably stole the tapes. It is from the sessions for the double white album, really different versions. It's an absolute rarity, well worth the five quid mate." Keith assured him.

"Can I write you a cheque? I don't have that sort of cash on me." The customer asked, pen already in hand.

"No mate. I don't have a bank account. In fact I don't even exist. I live on cash only. No records at all, except this lot of course, hahaha." Was our Philanthropist developing a sense of humour at long last?

"Oh. Well never mind, I'll have to leave it then. A pity, I really wanted that one. Maybe I'll come back next week."

"Yes, I'll keep it for you – but bring me cash next time."

"Maybe – we'll see." Keith knew he wouldn't return, you developed an instinct after a while. But he had lost a sale; he might have to do something about that.

And that evening he asked Joan about opening a bank account, what papers would he need. She explained that they would want to see some sort of proof of his address, and a personal recommendation from someone who had an account at the bank. Would she do that for him? Yes, okay. She supposed it would be okay, but don't go getting overdrawn and get me into trouble now. It was a strange relationship. Joan was still sleeping with him, but she had always had trouble trusting men, or rather trusting them too much. She liked Keith, but he was only a kid really and he wouldn't last, he would be off with someone younger soon enough; that might be a relief in a way. They were both dancing around each other, needing and liking the sex, but knowing that this light and airy time would never last. It would have to become something else soon. That had always happened before and she knew that when she started relying on men, that was when the trouble started. She remembered the bad times, the beatings, the degrading acts they had made her perform, the craving for cocaine that had driven her to do anything for money. She remembered being shared with so-called boyfriends friends, being laughed at, being abused. And she knew herself only too well too, that a part of her wanted this. She knew she had a fatal weakness for cruelty and dependence. She knew she had to avoid it and yet she wanted it too. Not that she thought Keith might be like that, but you never knew. With a man you never really knew; maybe it was something in her that made men *want* to hurt her. And Keith, or whoever he really was had been burned too. That was obvious and both of them, each in their own way, were wary of commitment, of getting in any deeper.

He moved out a few weeks after getting his bank account and found a bedsit a few streets away. It was quite amicable, they had talked about it. They had both known the relationship, if that was what it had been, was going nowhere. There was the age difference for a start. Sooner or later Keith would want someone younger. Joan did love him in a way, but she had been damaged by men in the past and wasn't going to lose everything again, especially for someone so young. He was bound to move on sometime anyway, and she wasn't surprised when he said he was thinking of getting his own flat. She didn't try to stop him; it was easier this way. Easy come, easy go, she rationalised to herself, but a part of her was sad. But she had learned to harbour her sadness, to cosset it, to use it as a blanket to keep herself warm. He promised to keep in touch, and did return a few times over the next few weeks. But they both knew it was just for the sex, he got up and left soon after, not even staying for a cup of tea. It reminded her of so many men in the past who just wanted to get away as soon as possible, where minutes before they had been whispering how much they loved her. Maybe they both accepted that that was okay too.

Keith James soon started building up a healthy balance at the bank. He paid money in every week and the bank must have thought he had a regular job. Almost everyone was paid in cash in those days so no-one asked to see any proof he was working. He was careful with his chequebook, paying his rent and a few times for things from shops, but he never went anywhere near overdrawn or agreed any Standing Orders. He kept his own records, the daily takings on his stalls and anything he spent, in a large blue foolscap book. The bank was safer than having a lot of cash around and was handy for those few people who wanted to pay by cheque.

Then the idea came to him. If it had been so easy opening a bank account for Keith James, how easy it would become to open one in a different name. He had plenty of ready cash so he started renting another room in Kentish town in the name of Robert Johnson (an old blues singer from the twenties) and after a few weeks walked into a different branch and applied for a bank account for his new persona. He used the highly respectable Keith James as his reference. As soon as he had the second account he moved out of the flat in Kentish Town and two months later Peter Weston had a new bank account as well. He kept all three accounts well stocked with money, and wrote occasional cheques on each account. So now he had three identities, three people he could possibly become. Without even trying he was gaining a degree of acceptability, a toehold in the system he despised. He wasn't really sure what he needed them for, but the subterfuge, the element of deceit, excited him. Just like mixing up the orders on his paper round or pasting Lady Chatterley into hymn books he was subtly altering the world around him. Besides you never knew …

He started two more market stalls with these new names, one at Angel Islington and another in the Portobello road, he had no real choice, business was booming. He had to employ staff, but that was easy, there were plenty of young guys who wanted to work for cash. He moved stock around, and was meticulous about keeping records. He would sit up late at night checking what had been sold and making sure his staff weren't nicking money (well not too much anyway, he knew they would look after the stall if they could slip a few pounds their own way each week). He pulled them up if they exceeded his unwritten limits and was quick to lose any really greedy workers. And it worked remarkably well; it was an unwritten contract – the first of many. He filled up book after book with numbers, and was secretly excited at how the money in the bank accounts was building up. Within a year he had over a thousand pounds. Three years ago he had thought three hundred a lot of money, now he knew that even thousands would not really be enough. He didn't want money for anything specific, not yet. But he knew that if he really wanted to avoid detection, to live outside the law, without a real identity, to be on no government records, to be free to become a new person whenever he needed then he would need money and lots of it. Money could buy you anything; it was the one thing the world really respected. He still lived frugally, only buying clothes when he had to. He had all the books and records he ever wanted, and when he tired of them he would sell them on.

Occasionally he thought back to the old reel-to-reel he had, and had been forced to leave behind at Stoke Newington. He had always loved taping, from the radio or Top of the Pops, and now he had all these records in front of him. He bought himself a cassette player, the latest thing, the man in the store explained, you would be able to buy pre-recorded tapes soon, but could just as easily record straight from a record deck as long as you had an amplifier with phono-lead plugs. So he bought one of those as well. Now he spent every evening taping records onto cassettes, and built up a big collection, and it all cost practically nothing as he was selling on the albums anyway.

He even hit on the idea of making compilations, of rarities and singles of hard-to-find bands, or bootlegs and selling those on his stalls. He typed out the labels meticulously; then a girl he met told him she could photocopy them at her college, and make them pretty and colourful. She was an Art student, and willingly created the designs for him. He never considered this as theft. He was simply filling a gap in the market, providing fans with stuff they couldn't get through the conventional record shops. Okay, so the artists weren't getting royalties, but he reasoned that they were all being ripped off by the record companies anyway, and the more stuff he put out the more the fans might buy the official albums. But in truth it never really bothered him that much. Money in the bank interested him more. And he thrived; he only spent what he had to and saved the rest. He opened a few Building Society Accounts too. All you needed there was a name and address, and as these were savings accounts and you couldn't overdraw there was less security. He slowly transferred cash into these accounts, and carried the pass books around with him at all times.

But something was niggling at him. This whole enterprise was very flaky. Sooner or later the taxman might catch up with him, questions might be asked by the market inspectors or the banks. He might be asked for a birth certificate or some other proof of identity. Dylan had sung "to live outside the law you must be honest" and Keith knew he must start to become someone. Someone real. He couldn't just keep on making up names and moving flat every few months. Sooner or later he might slip up. And how would he ever explain away the different names and accounts and chequebooks and all of that.

And like serendipity the solution came looking for him rather than him having to seek it out. This smartly dressed man in his thirties turned up one day at his stall in Camden Town. Keith liked working here himself. It was where he had started and he had a good regular clientele. Here he was Keith, everyone knew him; he felt safe without being trapped. This man was different from his usual customers, a bit older and he wore a suit for a start, a bit crumpled but a suit. When he spoke it was from a different world, more cultured, not exactly a posh accent, but definitely well-spoken. Keith realised this be-suited man wasn't really interested in the albums as he flicked through them nonchalantly with his fingers; he wasn't really looking at the covers, just going through the motions. Something told him though that this might be an opportunity, something about the way he kept glancing at him. He waited until they were alone and he looked at and held eye contact with the strange man. Keith was about to say something when the stranger himself spoke.

"I've heard about you. Keith, isn't it? Not that that's your real name. I don't believe that for a minute." He said, his smile belying the almost threat of his words.

"Who's been talking about me then?" Keith, a bit alarmed, replied.

"Oh, you know, word gets around." Again that smile that hovered permanently a few inches apart from whatever he was saying.

"Does it really?" said Keith sarcastically, "So, what *have* you heard about me? And can I ask your name, as you seem to know mine."

"Sure, but mine is just about as genuine as yours. Shall we just say you can call me Bob." The smile was disarming. How could you get angry with a smile like that, but it certainly was irritating.

"Okay Bob, and what brings you here. You don't want to buy any records; that's for sure."

"No. To tell the truth it all sounds much the same to me. Call me a philistine but music, this modern stuff anyway, doesn't excite me at all."

"What does then? Why are you here at all, Bob?" Keith knew that this Bob was serious, for a moment he thought he may be Police or some sort of taxman, but why the admission that he too had a false name.

"Cars. Yes. Cars excite me, not music." His smile was massive now, almost a laugh.

"Cars?" Keith was surprised, that was the last thing he had been expecting.

"Yeah, motors. Motors interest me. Selling them - not necessarily driving them mind you. Lots of money in selling cars, you know. Makes this look like chicken feed I can tell you." And he disdainfully dismissed the stall stacked full of records in cardboard boxes with a wave of his cuff-linked hand.

"So what are you suggesting? I don't even drive."

"I thought we might go into business, you and me. I've been watching you for a while. Three markets you are on now, that's right isn't it? And you use a different name on each. And I bet you don't pay a penny in tax on any of them." Bob had suddenly stopped smiling and his gaze was cool as ice.

"Look, just who the fuck are you mister?" Keith was really worried now, who was this smart dressed and smart-tongued guy who knew so much about him? Trouble, he knew that much for sure.

"Don't be so defensive, I'm not the law." The smile had returned. "And I don't want to take anything from you. I'm not interested in your little business at all, but sooner or later this is all going to go up in smoke; if the taxman doesn't get you, the police will, or some protection gangsters or other." Bob reached in his pocket and took out a packet of American Marlboro. Waving them at Keith who declined, he continued between puffs "You are making far too much money and people get jealous I've found. Human nature; they hate success. At some point you are going to have to get legit, or you're going to come a cropper, as they say." Exhaling through his nostrils Bob smiled again, "I'm actually trying to help you, I may just be your escape route out of here my boy."

"So what are you after? What's in it for you? Why should I listen to you rather than anyone else? How do I know you don't just want to muscle in and take over my patch?"

"You don't. And actually I really do not want to steal your livelihood. Just look at me." And he opened his arms wide to show his pin-stripe three-piece suit and crisp white shirt. "Can you imagine me working on a market stall? But actually I am offering you something else completely. I want you to join me. Selling cars. Only this is one hundred percent legitimate. I pay my taxes and abide by all the rules (or most of them anyway). Only I make a hell of a lot more money than you do, or ever will I might add. I am, in short, offering you a job Keith."

"And why should I work for you when I have my own business here?"

"Meet me in the George at six and I'll show you why. Oh I forgot you don't drink, do you Keith. Better make it that little cafe over there. Six, okay?" He flicked the half-smoked cigarette at his feet and stubbed it out with a highly polished brogue shoe.

Keith was about to speak but Bob had turned on his rather elegant black shoes and walked away without a glance back. This stranger, this Bob, had really upset Keith. Who was this guy, and how did he know so much about him? He knew about his three identities and Keith had never told a soul about them. He must have been watching him, asking after him, and if he had been asking questions among the other stall-holders how much did he really know? Did he know about the multiple bank accounts? Did he know his real name, the one nobody in London knew; surely Keith had covered his tracks well enough? But he was excited as well as worried. He had known too that one day he might be rumbled, but he had suspected the authorities in some shape or form; the Police, or someone from the local council. But this guy said he sold cars. He had offered Keith a job. What sort of a job? Keith knew nothing about cars; he wasn't interested in cars at all. But he was intrigued. This Bob (an alias just as Keith was his surely) had talked about going legitimate. How exactly would that be accomplished, and how would it feel too? He had enjoyed making up names, it was easy, but apart from a rent book and a bank account he still had no papers at all. Could he just keep running all his life? Was this just another trap opening up invitingly in front of him? Or was it a way forward? Keith would have to be careful, he would have to make sure he could trust this Bob. Or, actually know that he could never trust him, but maybe he could use him. It wouldn't hurt to meet him anyway, would it?

Wembley

Keith started working with Bob a couple of months later. Or rather James Pilkington went into business with Richard Moore; co-directors of 'SuperAutoTraders' of Wembley. Richard told him he would have to smarten up too; get his hair cut and lose the beard. Crisp white shirts, three-piece suit and tie would be replacing the T-shirts and jeans. Keith was informed that if he wanted to go legit he would have to drop the name of his choice and get a real one. There was a small choice of names available at any one time, but you couldn't just be any name you fancied. You could actually 'assume' the identity of a real person, but only a dead one - so at any one time there would only be certain names available. But Keith rather liked the name of James Pilkington, who in fact had died in a road accident in 1961, aged ten. So James would have been the perfect age for Keith to become him, and just as easily as he slipped his legs into the pin-striped and lined suit trousers he slipped into another person's skin. Bob, or Richard Moore as James now learned to call him, arranged it all. Richard knew people. Or he knew people who knew people who could organise it for him. One week and two hundred pounds later and James had his very own Birth Certificate and could now apply for a passport and a new bank account quite legally (or so it would appear, and that was all that really mattered).

Did our philanthropist ever think about the boy who had died, or how outraged his Mum and Dad would have felt if they knew he had stolen their dead son's identity? I doubt it, things were moving quickly now – he was on the up. Now he was official, now he was legit, as Richard called it. Getting a National Insurance number cost another hundred. If you knew people anything was possible, at a price.

But why him? Why had Richard chosen him, James, to be his new partner? Because he had been watching him and studying his operation for a while now, he recognised the same thing in Keith, as he was then, as he saw in himself; a natural ability to make money, a sharp intelligence and a streak of ruthlessness too. But why did Richard need him, if he could make money himself?

"Oh, my dear boy, do you not see? The more links in the chain before the money gets to me, links that can be broken and discarded if needed, the better. And actually the really clever people all surround themselves with other clever (and greedy) people who can and do make them even more money. You were only doing the same thing with your proxy stall-holders. We are just up-scaling from now on in. You will employ smart people to make you rich just as you (greedy boy) will make the money for me. Of course you will be well rewarded for your efforts, but I will be just as well rewarded without putting in the effort. My contribution is the idea and the capital to get you started." And again that smile hovering a few inches from the mouth that had spoken the words. "It really is as simple as that."

It was going to work like this: James would actually run the place day-to-day, keep the records, and most importantly make sure that no one was ripping them off.

"Don't take your eye off the ball for a second." Richard explained to James the night before they opened. "Check everything and then check again, and let your staff all know you are watching them. Better they should hate and be scared of you than think you are their mate and sooner or later end up stealing from you. I saw how you worked the kids running your other stalls; I saw the way they looked at you - that little gleam of fear. They knew that you were watching them, and that was enough to keep them in line." And dusting his shiny brogues with a small cloth he continued. "I suppose in a way I am taking a chance with you, James. But the one thing I am good at is judging people's character. I am pretty sure you and I will work out well together, but if we don't I can assure you that you will be the first to know. I told you that in many ways you had similar traits to me; one of those traits is ruthlessness." A different, almost sinister smile hovered now. "So, I too will be watching you and if I suspect you of letting me down or even thinking of ripping me off you will see just how utterly ruthless I can be. Let us hope you won't make me bring that particular one into play." And the old familiar smile returned as they shook hands. "But remember, it's only business. Nothing personal - you must understand."

In no time James was running the show and as far as the staff knew he was the only boss; Richard had two other car-showrooms to run and never showed up until late at night while James was alone and making up the books. James enjoyed this more than any other time of day; the concrete forecourt deserted, staff and customers all gone, cars all neatly parked facing the road, the dark night outside, the rain on the big glass windows, and James inside with his ledgers, writing up all the day's sales and expenses in separate columns. Somehow he knew he could trust these rows and columns of numbers far more than he would ever trust people. Richard had told him that you don't really need to know anything about selling cars at all. You didn't even have to like cars yourself.

"All you really need to know is how people react, how they behave, how they want to improve themselves, how to appeal to their desires, to their greed, how to make them think they are realising their dreams." Richard had explained at their first real meeting.

"Dreams?" James had said.

"Yes, dreams. That is what we are really selling here. Dreams, not cars." Richard had insisted. "Half of your punters won't have even passed their tests yet. Everyone wants a car, they think it will make them someone, friends will look up to them and women will sleep them – if they have a car. They all have their dreams. We are just the conduit; we are simply here to fulfil their little dreams."

And so James gave up his market stalls. Or not quite. He asked Jim, the guy who ran the stall at Angel, to run the other two for him as well. He arranged to meet him once a week, when Jim handed over the blue sales book and the money. James (Keith) knew that Jim would steal from him. The business was all cash and nothing is so easy to steal as cash. That was okay, as long as Jim didn't get too greedy. James knew exactly how much Jim was keeping for himself on top of his wages, but he didn't really mind. It kept him interested and kept him watching those beneath him, making sure they didn't nick too much either. He would occasionally drop a subtle hint that business was slow or sales a bit disappointing and next week they would bounce back up. After a couple of years he told Jim that he could have the business, lock stock and barrel.

"How much will that cost me?" Jim asked warily.

"Nothing Jim, I've just decided to give it to you. To tell the truth it's peanuts for me now and I can't afford the time to keep checking on it. You've been pretty honest these two years, and you need a break. Have fun." And they shook hands, as Keith smiled another life away. This was the last time he used the name Keith and incidentally it was his first real act of Philanthropy too.

James soon learned about the Car business. In a way it was the same as records. The secret was in the buying. People selling second-hand cars were usually desperate, especially for cash; bills to pay, debts piling up or simply downsizing. So it was easy to find fault with the vehicles, make out you didn't need another Austin Allegro on your forecourt, shake your head and gently kick the tyres, see the disappointment in their eyes and begin to walk away. Then stop, turn on your heel and walk back quickly with the hundred quid in your hand, push it into their palm and leaning in close say you'd take it off their hands for a ton.

Turnover. That was the key to the business, keep the tills ringing, keep the cars moving, don't let anything stand on the forecourt too long. Punters will come back if they see new cars every week. Sell, sell, sell. Even at a loss sometimes, just keep things moving, keep a steady but ever-changing stream of shiny cars on show and people would start to go there, because nothing succeeds like success. People will buy from a successful trader because he must know what he is doing. Even if what he was really doing was fleecing people. But the customers were unaware, they left SuperAutoTraders happy. Happy owners of their dreams, or with ready cash in their pockets and that old rust-bucket gone at last. It was as simple as that. Keep everyone happy, that was the trick. James paid high wages to his salesmen, and commission on top of that. His staff, even the girls in the back office, were happy and well rewarded, but he was also merciless and got rid of anyone underperforming or trying to steal with no hesitation at all. And publicly, that was the secret. Let the others know you are ruthless, that despite being younger than them, no-one could take you for a ride. And so the business thrived.

They moved to bigger premises, a prime spot on the High Road with lots of footfall as people passed to the bright new Tesco Supermarket next door. He took on more staff, everyone wore smart suits and white shirts and dark blue ties. and they sold even more cars.

Everyone wanted a car. When James was a child hardly anyone in their town had owned a car, now everyone wanted one. And with inflation racing away better to buy one now before the prices go up again. And SuperAutoTraders was completely legitimate, they broke no laws, their Accounts were audited, they happily paid their taxes. And the two directors toasted each other with Champagne at their monthly board meetings, held in the private dining room of Wembley's finest curry house (James drinking strictly one glass only, the memory of all those 'alkie' dropouts he had seen when he was on the streets himself still haunted him).

James still lived quite frugally, saving almost all of his wages; he had a small flat in Wembley and walked to work each day. He worked long hours and even went in on a Sunday to go over the figures one more time. He never went out, on his own or with women, preferring his own company and his records at night. He had bought the flat, again on the advice of Richard, for a few thousand pounds and it had almost doubled in value in the two years since '75. Incredible, but inflation was in double figures and house prices were racing ahead of that. You couldn't lose, or so it seemed.

"We should really get into real estate." Richard suggested late one evening as James pored over the Sales dockets.

"Buying houses, you mean? Surely this can't last; my flat has practically doubled in price in two years. That can't carry on, can it?" James was always a bit sceptical of new ideas.

"Who knows James? But, no I think buying and selling property may be a little risky at the moment. The price of oil has almost trebled this year, things are hardly predictable. No-one knows how long Callaghan can hold this Government together, the Liberals are notoriously flaky. No, I mean we should think about becoming Estate Agents ourselves. You earn your commission whatever the price of houses, and if the price starts dropping maybe people will want to buy them quick before the price goes up again. I think houses might soon become like cars, the thing everyone wants."

"What about the car business? We are doing so well on that, we can't drop that surely?" James hesitantly said, he wasn't at all sure of becoming an estate agent.

"No. But we'll find someone to run that for us, just as I found you James. I couldn't have done it all on my own, so I found you. Or we might sell out completely; I've had a few decent offers. Maybe getting out of motors and into houses is the right move. But we are going to need a fair bit of capital to start with."

"How much are you talking about? I've got nearly thirty grand, give or take."

"I am not suggesting we use our own money James. That might be foolhardy. We need to borrow, and borrow big if we are at all serious. We need premises, shop-fronts, and lots of them, and glossy brochures and full page ads in the press. That will all cost money, and before we've sold a single house too. I reckon we need over a mill, maybe two - to do the job properly, that is."

James took a deep breath. "That is one hell of a lot of money Richard. Who has that sort of money?"

"The banks, my boy, that's who. But first we need a business plan, and an Accountant and a decent lawyer. A whole new company in fact. I can only offer you ten percent. If you want in that is. Twenty grand for your shares and in no time the business could be worth a few million, ten percent of which will be yours. Sound good?" The famous smile was hovering in the air.

"And if it doesn't work? If we go broke?" James, always the realist, asked.

"Then it's cost you twenty thousand, and you can walk away. We will be a limited company; all we will lose is our start-up costs. The bank will take the loss. That's the beauty of the thing. And hell, we might just have fun with this one. I'm tired of cars, aren't you?" Richard closed the ledger and he and James walked out into the cool night air, full of dreams, hopes and dreams of being millionaires.

Marylebone

The headquarters, the grand showroom and the main office, of Move-on-up was in Marylebone. Just to the North and the West of Oxford Street but very plush, very swish. Smart Edwardian mansion blocks, tree-lined Avenues and smart trendy boutiques; this was miles away from Stoke Newington or Wembley's windswept car-lots. Richard and James wore hand-tailored three-piece suits, handmade shoes and gold cuff-links and tie-pins. Nothing breeds success like success so they had to be dressed for the part; like actors in a play they were writing themselves into the script of the rich boys and maybe relied too much on expensive props, but the banks fell over themselves to lend them money and then when they needed to expand they were tapped up for even more cash. It was as if money was no object, the more they asked for the more important and successful they must be. And the bigger the loans the more plush the showrooms the more sales they clocked up; rich clients it seemed liked their estate agents to look as rich as they were themselves. The loans were huge and from several banks and investment vehicles, but repayments were made promptly, and Richard even insisted on paying back some of the smaller loans early to impress the bankers (only to be used as collateral for even larger loans of course). James was finance director and stayed late every night writing up the books. It was much the same as in the car showroom and before that the market-stall, only the numbers just had more noughts on them.

In 1982 they bought their first computer, it cost a couple of thousand pounds and was heavy, cumbersome and slow but James was enthralled with Lotus 123, the spreadsheet facility. He had always loved numbers, the way they always added up, they never let you down. Their solidity, their reliability; unlike people - you could always trust numbers. And now he had the computer with its fuzzy green digits on a black screen, clunking along to make sure the numbers always added up. James was amazed – it only took seconds to add whole columns and rows, and you could save it all onto floppy discs too, so you never lost anything. For at least a year though James still filled in the large foolscap blue books and cross-checked with the IBM, and once or twice they didn't balance, only to find on rechecking that it was always his own arithmetic that was in error. After a few early mornings re-adding his own handwritten columns and finding his mistake, usual a transposed number, he learned to trust the computer.

So, the Philanthropist was now becoming wealthy by anyone's standards surely. Only eight years ago he was homeless and now had many thousands of pounds in his various bank accounts. He soon sold his flat in Wembley and bought a smaller place, again for cash, in the smarter streets behind Baker Street. Smaller; but far more exclusive and a lot more expensive too. As he began to understand real estate he was still amazed that location was far more important than size, and he was indeed the proud owner of a fully paid-for one bedroom pied-a-terre in a very exclusive mews at the back of a row of grandiose imposing white portico-ed Georgian town houses facing onto Regents Park. And it was here that he indulged himself somewhat. He bought a Bang and Olufsen stereo unit, with a vertical record deck; perspex and brushed steel that glided open with the slightest of touches. It had an amplifier with a whole array of sliding switches to control the base and treble and a separate cassette deck and radio receiver. He still had boxes of LPs from his market stall days and even more cassettes. He occasionally listened to new music but preferred the records he knew from the sixties and early seventies. He never talked about his music, nobody knew about this passion. It was for his ears only; after the day's work, late at night he would sit in his new black leather armchair, speakers either side of him and dissolve, disappear into the music. He limited himself to buying one new, but usually an old release, record a week and would wander down Baker Street to HMV on Oxford Street every Saturday afternoon and spend two or three hours browsing the racks, seeking out obscure bands or old records that had somehow passed him by.

And some nights he would wander out late at night and pick up a prostitute. The fact that Joan had confessed that she had been one for a while had always fascinated him. What was it that made this oldest of all trades so intriguing to him? Was it the element of control? Or the dispassionate uninvolved nature of the transaction; none of that falling in love business, this was purely a set price, negotiated in advance, for his satisfaction. There was no consideration even whether the girl, the prostitute, was enjoying it; in fact the secret knowledge that they probably hated it was in itself quite thrilling. The first time he had done this, picked up a street girl, he had almost chickened out. He had watched quietly from the other side of the road as the girls outside Paddington station had plied their trade; all heavy make-up and short skirts and silly little handbags and tiny tops, no matter the cold weather. Silently watching but without quite having the nerve to approach them. The anticipation was exhilarating in itself, the possibility that he might return to his flat without having crossed this particular Rubicon. Once or twice one had nodded at him, trying to establish eye-contact, convert him from a watcher into a punter; but he had turned and walked quickly up the road a bit, pretending he wasn't interested but slowly returning to stand in some doorway and watch. Watching was almost as good as doing it himself. He was steeling himself, daring his own inner demon to do it. In the end it was one of the girls who approached him and asked casually if he was looking for a good time.

Silently he nodded and she said "You been standing here for ages 'aven't you? You ain't got a car, have you mister? I usually do the business in a car."

"No," He stuttered out, nerves almost stopping him from speaking at all, "but I don't live far away."

"I don't go back to blokes homes. Too dangerous. Know what I mean? But I know a place just round the corner. No-one can see us there. Okay?"

And again he nodded and looking around he followed a few yards behind her, pretending not to be following but making sure he didn't lose sight of her either, watching as the tight skirt rode up around her thighs and her arse wobbled enticingly with each step she took. He was nervous, but excited too. It had been a long time since Joan. Joan had been safe, but he had stopped going there a few years ago. He had enjoyed the sex though, maybe too much on reflection. Another addiction he was fearful of falling into; he had moved out because he had been scared he might end up falling for her. She had helped him and she was kind and loving, even if she was a lot older than him. He had started looking forward to seeing her, to fucking her to be precise, but he was determined never to fall in love again (or at least not so soon, not so deeply, not so disastrously). So he had avoided having girlfriends or even casual dates, but he had thought about it more than a few times since then. A couple of the secretaries at the office had made eyes at him, asked him if he was coming out with everyone to the pub after work. They had leaned over his desk in their low tops and short skirts and he had been tempted, he had to admit. It was all too obvious what they were offering, but he knew how dangerous it would be to screw one of the office girls; jealousies and grudges would be harboured, and besides he just wanted uncomplicated sex, no involvement, no dinner dates, no wooing, no becoming boy and girlfriend. He had done that once and look how badly it had ended. So, though flattered he had stopped himself. He knew instinctively that any carrying on with the admittedly gorgeous girls at work would mean trouble. So he always smiled politely and said no, he was too busy. The accepted wisdom was that he must be a queer, and he rather liked this assumption, his own inner knowledge at variance with the common perception. At least he wasn't bothered so much as time went on and any new girls were told they were wasting their time on that one.

The young woman looked back as she turned into an alleyway between two shops. She walked right to the end, where she was almost lost in the darkness of the overhanging walls, and turned to face him. No light from the street reached this far, she held his arm and he felt almost as much as heard as she whispered into his ear.

"Okay love, what do you want? I don't do sex without a condom or anal at all. Do you want a blow-job? That's fifteen, or sex is twenty."

"A blowjob I suppose" James mumbled out, he hadn't thought about the items on the menu, he just wanted some sex.

It didn't last long; she was very proficient and didn't waste any time. The quicker they came, the sooner she would be back on her patch. But even so it was still incredibly thrilling for James. He loved the excitement, the danger, the possibility of being seen, the sheer naughtiness of the thing, the anonymity; the fact that it was so out of character for him. Nobody at work would ever have guessed that he was out here, standing up, his back against the grimy wall as this pretty young woman wrapped her lips round him. He looked down the alleyway and saw people scurrying by unaware that he was being sucked off just yards from them. He closed his eyes as he came and seconds later she leaned over and spat the gob of his come onto the litter-strewn ground. He zipped up his flies and walked away from her quickly as she stopped under a street light to re-apply her lipstick. He felt elated, almost ecstatic, but slightly guilty too - a strange mix. He kept looking over his shoulder as he walked hurriedly back to his luxury apartment, just checking that no-one had seen him, that he wasn't being followed; though rationally why should he be - it didn't stop this strangely oppressive feeling, the awareness that he had crossed a line somehow, an unwritten rule that separated him from most other men who had girlfriends, fiancées or wives and wouldn't dream of paying for a prostitute. Or so he imagined in his panicky flight back to the safety of his home.

Back in the flat he couldn't quite believe he had done it. It was one of those taboo things, men never talked to each other about it. Or none had ever admitted such a thing to him. Football, cars and drinking were the things he noticed that men talked about at work. He hardly knew anything about any of those three, but had learnt the knack of smiling and nodding and agreeing with them. Most people he discovered simply liked the sound of their own voice and if you silently agreed with them, nodding every now and then, they quite enjoyed this form of conversation; very few really liked to listen. Besides he didn't ever feel he had much to say to these young men, so confident, so brash, so cocky really; he was their boss and though friendly he would never be their friend. In fact of course he had no friends at all, except maybe Richard, but he wasn't even sure if Richard could be considered a friend. There was always a studied distance with Richard. He had maybe had friends at school but had somehow lost the knack of acquiring them since then. Richard and a few of the top people in the office talked business, bar charts and the unexplainable vagaries of the erratic luxury housing market. But never about sex, or explicitly about this sort of thing; prostitutes, buying it. A few jokes about who had the best tits in the office was as far as they ever went. And for James keeping it secret was almost as exciting as doing it. The fact that nobody knew what he was up to made it so excruciatingly pleasurable. His dirty little secret. But then it was all a secret, his real identity, his records, his sex life. It was all part of the same thing; this intensely secret life which nobody knew a thing about. He had always known he could hide himself away in London and even as a successful businessman he was still hiding himself away. The real him was always hidden, that's how he liked it. And the knowledge that nobody guessed a thing about him, his love of music, his secret world of buying sex were his and his alone.

And once he had broken this taboo, it became far too easy. Once a week he would 'treat' himself. He soon moved from street girls, (far too dangerous, far too exposed) to escorts. Printed cards had started appearing in phone-boxes all over London's West End advertising call-girls or models as they liked to be called, and pretending to make a call he would peel a couple off the wall and slip them into the silk-lined jacket of his suit. This was a much easier arrangement, ringing up a faceless number at midnight and trying to guess from the voice just what she might be like. Then arranging for her to come to his flat; the element of surprise as he opened his front door; would she be blonde or brunette, chubby or thin, black, white or tan, and even the possibility that he might turn her away (with a tenner for her trouble) if she didn't appeal to him. But that had only happened once or twice, the girls were usually astonishingly attractive. He loved the feeling that he was in total control, she was there for his pleasure alone. He was paying her and she was there to do whatever turned him on, though as we have all discovered there isn't that much in the repertoire that is really different - except the face.

Then all of a sudden things started to go wrong. The bank started to get nervous, a few months of flat sales, interest rates rising, they had overstretched themselves. Some branches were underperforming badly. Richard blamed James - he was the Finance Director after all.

He had taken his eye off the ball, why hadn't he spotted this trend earlier. They rapidly closed a few branches and sacked some staff, but sales kept slipping, cash-flow got worse, bills went unpaid and they remained in trouble. They took no wages themselves for a couple of months and still the business was barely breaking even, let alone able to repay loans. The banks started asking for their money back. An emergency board meeting was convened and Directors whom James had barely heard of decided they must sell the business for what they could get for it. But times were bad and they barely scraped their way out of it. They still owed the Government a couple of hundred thousand in unpaid VAT, and the banks only got half their money back. Richard walked unsmiling away from the solicitor's office without shaking James's hand. It had all been done in such a hurry, a panic really that had overwhelmed them, and James felt he was being made the scapegoat. He was being blamed but was never really in control, of the company - let alone events. Richard had been the one pulling the strings, negotiating ever larger loans from the banks, assuring him it would all be okay, this was how business was done; he was just there to sign the papers and do the books. James phoned him later that night.

"Well, I'm sorry you feel that way old boy. We made a bit of money for a while, but the big boys muscled in on us I'm afraid. Too much competition; and we were squeezed out of the market. These things happen; it's the nature of business. You must learn not to hold grudges." Richard was remarkably cool about it all. "Never apologise, never admit defeat – they taught us that at school. Just smile and walk away – it's only business after all."

"So, what happens next, Richard? I mean is this the end of our friendship?" James suddenly realised he had no job and no friend to help him this time.

The Philanthropist

"Friendship, James? I think you may be misunderstanding things a bit. Look, I pulled you out of a market stall in Camden. I liked your operation, small as it was. I thought you had potential and for a while it worked, for a while we did well, but there was never any friendship I can assure you of that. It was purely business. I am sorry if you fooled yourself into thinking that it was anything approaching friendship old boy." And he laughed, he actually laughed at the idea that James, a scruff from Camden Market, could ever be counted amongst his friends; why, he didn't even go to the same school.

"But what about the car business, we did well there didn't we?" James was sounding a bit too desperate now.

"Yes, and maybe we should have stayed selling cars, but there you go, we didn't. Look, no hard feelings or anything but I think it best we go our own way for a while, don't you?"

"Is that it then? Is that all there is?" James was upset now at this cursory dismissal, after all he had worked his socks off for Richard who was hardly ever at the office himself.

"Look James, you are a bright boy, but to be honest you let me down. I wasn't going to tell you this but perhaps it's better you hear it from me than from others. I thought you were a bit smarter than you were, but you weren't quick enough to spot the downturn when it happened. You don't quite have that edge I thought you might have. When the chips were down so were you. You floundered a bit and lost your nerve; maybe I should have kept a closer eye on things myself but you were the whizz-kid, you were the man with the computer, you should have been smarter. I have nothing against you personally but I think this is the end of our relationship, for the present at least. I never hold grudges in business, you never know when you will need people again, but let's just leave it there, shall we?"

"If you say so, Richard" James was stunned at this analysis, shocked to think that Richard thought he was a failure. All he could say was "Goodbye, then."

"Goodbye James. And good luck for the future."

So, within the space of six months the business, their glorious empire had collapsed. James had earned a good salary for a few years, and had a nice flat and a wardrobe full of expensive clothes. But he had no job. He had never quite understood the nature of business, how you eventually had to start turning a decent profit, borrowing money from the banks was okay while you were growing but when things turned bad the banks would always squeeze you hard. He had been lucky. Lucky with the market stalls, lucky to meet Bob, or Richard or whatever his name was. Lucky with the car business and lucky for a while with real estate, and he simply assumed that it would all continue, that business was easy, that all you had to do was keep selling and you would succeed. But that had all come to an end and rather a sharp and nasty end too. James was hung out and on his own. He really knew no-one except Richard. The other Directors were there for show, they never came to the office, he just saw them at the monthly board meetings, a quick shake of the hand and they were off to another meeting somewhere else, another company, another board meeting, another handshake. But when it came to it, they seemed to be the ones making the big decisions. James was sidelined, his graphs and spreadsheets ignored. Decisions were taken by others and he was shown where to sign. This wasn't the world he had been born into. Though he wore the right suits he wasn't a natural businessman. He hadn't gone to the right schools and he wasn't even ruthless enough when it came to it. He should have acted quicker when he saw sales falling off. He thought it was just a blip; that the market would bounce back. And he didn't like sacking people; he knew all the staff by name, he worked with them. He had wanted to wait, ride out the storm. He was too slow in closing down unprofitable offices; he didn't really understand the business. Richard was right; he wasn't as smart as he thought he was.

He was down alright but certainly not out. He was on his own now, but maybe that was a good thing too. Richard had known him when he ran a market stall in Camden, when he called himself Keith; everyone else had a different idea of him. Richard had known he had bought his identity, purchased a dead boy's birth certificate and re-invented himself. No-one else knew that, from now on he could lose that connection completely. Re-invent himself once more? Maybe take on a new identity once more, but actually James Pilkington had been rather good to him. Better hang on to whatever creditability that name had earned him for a while. He still had his rather luxurious flat and several thousand pounds in quite an array of bank accounts, some still under his old aliases. So what next? He had to get a job, the flat was paid for and he had money in the bank, but he had never forgotten how stupid he had been when he first came to London and had let his savings slip through his fingers, blinded by love as he might have been. He always remembered sleeping on flattened out cardboard boxes and going hungry and unwashed for weeks, existing on charity handouts. Mustn't let that happen again. All in all things weren't that bad. Maybe I should celebrate, get a girl in. Only a hundred pounds and you never saw them again, that was the beauty of it. You fucked them and then they fucked off. No trap at all. And now he was free of Richard maybe that was another trap he had escaped from.

He slipped an old Stones album on the Bang and Olufsen, shut his eyes and tried not to worry. 'Paint it Black' – if only he could.

The City

He thought about things for a few days. He had a lot going for him. He knew how to wear a suit (long gone now those t-shirts and jeans), he could talk business, he knew the jargon, the buzz-words, he understood numbers, he had money in the bank and his own flat paid for. Should he go into business on his own? He knew enough about how to start up a company, and how to tap up the banks for finance. But doing what exactly? Selling cars and houses, he knew about that alright, but his experiences with Richard had soured him. For a while he toyed with returning to selling records on a market stall, he had been happy then at least. But the idea faded, he just couldn't see himself doing that again. He fancied something different; he needed a challenge, some way of proving if only to himself that he was good at this world of business. Richard's parting comments had really hurt him - he wouldn't forget that in a long time. It was '85 and the Tories had just liberated the City. The Big Bang they called it, suddenly all the old rules that had stood for maybe hundreds of years were being torn up. Anyone could work in the City now. It wasn't necessary to have trained as a stockbroker for years, or know about finance at all really. Being quick on your feet, knowing your way around a computer, working long hours, seizing opportunities, spotting mugs; that was what it was all about.

He decided to go to an upmarket Employment Agency, they helped write his CV (he had never needed one before), he invented the schools, schools he had heard his fellow Directors mention, and nobody ever asked to see his three 'A' levels. He was welcomed with open arms. He had run his own business after all, been a Director already, just the sort of person the City were looking for. He went for an interview at a new company, an investment house that had just set up near Mansion House. They were looking for senior staff, people who knew about money, people who knew how to wear a decent suit; who could talk the talk and walk the walk. He got the job without really trying. Yes, they had heard of Move-on-up, he had sold at just the right time apparently. When could he start? Straightaway? Why not? Welcome aboard. He was part of a team seeking out and wooing new clients, trying to get them to invest in their funds. Health was the growing market. Private healthcare, health insurance, pharmaceuticals, these were the new wealth-makers; they were outstripping all other sectors and by investing in the right companies, by diversifying their portfolio they could always outperform the market (or so the story went). There were plenty of rich new clients out there wanting to invest in shares, they just needed some assistance, and our investment house was just the place to come to. Our associates worked with the clients to design the best portfolio for them, one that gave a degree of security along with the excitement of a few high fliers. And along the way the fees kept going up and everyone (well, us really) got richer and richer.

James had his own comfortable office and a secretary who arranged the appointments and two bright young junior associates who handled the paperwork. James's job was to talk to the clients, to entertain them, to soften them up, to get them to invest. Here among some of the oldest buildings and tiny dark passageways the City of London was modernising at speed; large skyscrapers were rising like shiny new beasts, seemingly out of place they would soon become accepted and dwarfed by even taller monoliths in a few years, as the voracious City ate itself. And he liked the work, he was good at it. He let people talk; he took his time with clients, giving them the illusion that they were in control while all the time he was guiding them in his own direction. Selling the dream again; just like cars, just like houses. Unit Trusts were no different. Everyone wanted to get rich, didn't they? But they didn't want the risk, they needed someone to buy and sell for them, to watch the market every day, to decide when to sell and when to buy. And James was a good talker too; he made his clients feel relaxed. He was never pushy, in fact his best selling point was that when he saw that a client was dying to sign up, he would say.

"Look, think it over for a couple of days. Give me a ring after the weekend. Talk it over with your wife. Let me know what you decide. It's your money after all."

And that was the sucker punch. Nobody really thought about it over the weekend, all they thought was that the opportunity might slip through their grubby little fingers if they left it too long. Everyone was getting into shares, the banks paid crap interest. The last thing they would do was talk it over with their wives. Durgghh !!! And so he sealed the deal by appearing not to be at all bothered about sealing it. By not seeming particularly concerned, by asking the client to take his time he reassured them and at the same time hurried them into the only decision they were ever going to take. The clients thought he was a bit slow, not much of a salesman, but actually he was the best. He soon became the leading salesman in the business and was getting invites from other Investment houses. "How about lunch, just a general chat, no pressure." And he went along with them, listened to their schpeel, nodded and said he would think about it. Then he would talk to his bosses, let them know discreetly that he was 'hot' in the market, and in no time at all he was made a Director, given more money and shares in the business too. He was too good to let go to the opposition. This was a competitive business, good salesmen were like gold-dust; you had to hang onto them. Besides they were making so much money they could afford to make room at the top-table for such a valuable asset to the business.

But even with all this success James had his doubts. What did this so-called success amount to actually? He knew he was conning people really. The business was doing well, but the whole market was flying. It was almost impossible to fail. It wasn't that he had a conscience, he didn't actually feel guilty. People had their eyes open, or should have before they signed their money away. Anyway they were greedy and he felt no pity for the greedy. It just seemed a bit pointless really, this making money upon money. Both for himself, because he was on such a high salary anyway and commission on each new client he signed up, and for the clients and the company itself. Was making money an end in itself or was their more to life? What else he could do he really had no ideas, but he often looked back and remembered his attempt to be good, his bible studies, his desire to do good. He laughed at his naivety, but at least he had seen the trap that Religion was, only was this life, this richness, this lavish lifestyle not just as much a trap too. He often questioned himself, but for the time being it never really worried him that much. It was like a niggling tooth that only really bothered him when he probed too hard with his tongue; most of the time it was painless. But he was becoming more and more aware that his life was empty. Once he had liked it that way but now as he was getting older it began to worry him. Why was he on his own; everyone he knew had somebody, a wife a girlfriend, friends even. He had always been a loner, but now he was beginning to feel really alone.

While he had been building the businesses, records, cars and then houses with Richard – that had been an end in itself. That feeling of achieving something, of building a company, of making a success, of beating the competition, was thrilling and it had kept him going, the sense of achievement. This work was simply to make money and then more money. Of course like everyone he liked money, he liked the clothes, he liked being able to eat in smart restaurants, he moved into a larger flat in a better street, bought with cash again. There was no doubting the fact that he was successful, but what was it all for? He kept feeling that maybe he should get a partner, a wife even. Maybe children one day, who knew? Wasn't that what people did? Wasn't that what everyone did? Eventually. Okay so he had had his heart broken before he was twenty, but he was in his late thirties now. Maybe he could find love again. He certainly didn't love the escort girls. They satisfied a need, he enjoyed the feeling of power he had, that he could make them do almost anything if the money was right. He quite enjoyed the knowledge that they hated it, that they were only doing these things for the money he was willing to pay. That was a strange power, and quite addictive too. But Love? Hadn't that been his downfall before? Where had love got him last time? He remembered that coach journey up to and back from Edinburgh, and how his life might have ended up so differently if he had stayed with that first one. He remembered those two years sleeping rough in the streets around Waterloo; the perishing cold, the damp, the days spent lying in parks in the sun and thinking. He had come a long way since then, but what was it all for? Was his life really any more fulfilled now? His life was more comfortable he couldn't deny that, but in a strange way still as unfulfilled. He spent his nights sitting at home, brooding, listening to twenty year old records and musing on his life. Then in the morning he was up at six and at his desk by seven-thirty, on the phone by nine and wining and dining clients at lunch and often the evenings too. At least while he was busy there was no time to sit and think. But when he got home and looked around at all his comfortable things there was still that niggling question - what was it all for?

And maybe because he was in this mood anyway, maybe because he was just at the right age or maybe he was just ready, he started dating someone. She was actually a client, which of course was the last thing an Associate should ever do, that was an unwritten rule; never date the clients. Or rather she had nearly become a client; one of the few who turned him down and maybe in a way that was the attraction. She was a lawyer, a corporate lawyer working in the City too, helping clients during takeovers. Big money was involved, and she was part of a team of solicitors making sure the deals were done. She too was making good money and had heard that James was the man to go to for a sound but interesting investment. James had met her three or four times, expensive lunches and back in the office, but at the last minute she had decided not to go for it. No reason given, just not for her thanks. He had shrugged it off, 'you can't win 'em all', and moved on to the next client. Two weeks later she phoned James up and asked him to lunch.

"I thought you had decided not to invest with us Fiona. It is lovely to hear from you of course, but I am rather busy this week." He dissembled, he was always busy but for a potential client space could always be found.

"Look, just cut the crap for a minute will you. You are a damned good salesman James, but I wanted an opportunity to tell you just why I decided not to invest. And if you are too busy for lunch then how about dinner?" That was direct enough to send another message straight to the front of his mind.

"Okay. But I take it this is not strictly business." He replied, hesitant but certainly intrigued now.

"Let's just say I fancy dinner with you, and it would be an opportunity to keep in touch." (Red flag waving)

"In that case I would be delighted, how about tonight?" (responded the bull.)

And that was how it started. Fiona and James. He hadn't been expecting it at all. When she had been sitting opposite him he had seen how attractive she was, but that often happened and James never followed up, he had simply gotten out of the habit of chatting women up, if he had ever acquired it. It just wasn't something he did. But this was different, she had asked him out. And there was something in her voice, some hint of something more; he was intrigued and so, maybe against his better judgement, he had agreed. After all, it was only dinner, and perhaps he was fooling himself, maybe she did just want to tell him why she hadn't invested.

Marylebone and Islington

The dinner that night led to another - and then back to his flat and sex. Or actually this was more than sex. James wasn't paying for it, he wasn't even in control. Fiona was in control. He would discover later that she had always been in control. He had never really felt this way before, except at first with Joan, the woman with the past from Camden. He was used to being the instigator, the one who knew just what he wanted, the one in control and usually the one paying. He was being led, gently but certainly, with quiet authority and strangest of all he let himself be led. He who was always in control, he who never let his guard slip was suddenly the one being manipulated. He succumbed to her domination because it never felt like domination at all.

James knew, he realised what was happening but was simply unable to stop himself; he knew he was beginning to fall for her. This very attractive woman in her thirties was succeeding where all the pretty short-skirted secretaries had failed. She intrigued him; she was successful in her own right, intelligent and very much her own woman. She didn't need him, she made that quite clear – or not exactly, nothing was ever said, it was all inferred, she very cleverly kept him guessing. But he never felt that she really needed his love or indeed any emotional response from him, she seemed quite satisfied with his body. She didn't even pursue him, but still he couldn't stop thinking about her. He never quite understood what made her tick. She certainly loved success, winning both for her clients and for herself, and she won most of the time; there was very little time for losing at her high-end law firm. She loved money and what it could do for her, the smartest clothes, the best restaurants, her precious Mercedes, her very comfortable maisonette in Islington. But James was never sure if she felt the same for him as he was undoubtedly beginning to feel for her; he could never quite discern exactly what she was thinking about him. And this air of ambivalence she had, a sort of careless but at the same time studied nonchalance, as if she didn't in fact need him that much at all (but you never knew, did you), became for him the challenge, the very thing that he had to find out. It became a pursuit for him, almost an obsession, and strangely the harder he tried the less he felt sure he knew; in fact the more he tried to question her motives the more evasive and dismissive she became, kissing back his answers rather than directly replying, nibbling away his momentary doubts, until they would rise again, bobbing back to the surface of his mind like unwanted ghosts he struggled desperately to submerge. He feared that for her he might just be a passing fancy, a stop-gap, a mere dalliance; that this sexual bliss, this feeling of ecstasy he felt might end whenever she rose from his bed and dressed. As she closed her car door and drove off after that first night all these fears came to his mind, she never even waved at him as he stood watching from his bedroom window. He knew he was falling but whether simply into infatuation or into love or even into a void he wasn't quite sure. Sometimes he discerned the gentlest of sounds as the trap was closing over him, but then again it might just be his imagination. It was the uncertainty, her vagueness, her air of ambiguity that was hooking him deeper and deeper into this comfortable abyss, her most whimsical of nets.

She was the first woman he had even felt anything for since that first disastrous love of his. Sometimes he couldn't even remember her name, that first one, just the way she blinked her love back at him, wide-eyed and desperately clinging to him. Joan had been comfortable and comforting and gentle and oh so kind, but he had never loved her; he had been glad when he stopped seeing her, when the temptation was over.

There had been so many escort girls since, the faces and the bodies becoming interchangeable, even black and white merging into one unforgettable unknown and amorphous female body. He always asked their names at the door as they smiled at him so sweetly, but he had forgotten them by the time they were undressing or as they hastily tucked the money away in their handbags; and for sure in this seedy world no-one, even James of course, was using their real names anyway. He had changed his own name so often that names really had no meaning anymore. That first love had been such a long time ago too, almost half his life away; he had been a different person then, one even he now struggled to recall. Maybe forgetting was all part of the healing process, he could still remember her fair hair though and the way it used to fall over her eyes and the way she blinked through those wispy strands, and he would surely never forget that long bus journey all the way to Edinburgh and back again, but he couldn't really remember that much about her, the girl herself, who she really was or even how much he must have hurt her. He refused to think about her probable abortion or the life she might have gone on to lead after him, the boyfriends, the husband, the children she would most likely have by now or even if she still sometimes thought about him too. Better not to recall those desperate days, those sad lovelorn days. It was all a blur somehow; all he could really recall was that sickening feeling of lonely sadness as he wiped away the condensation from his own breath with the side of his hand and stared out of the bus window into that dark and rainy night.

Maybe he had never really known anything about her; maybe this had always been his problem. He thought he understood people, he thought he knew about human nature, he thought he knew how to manipulate people, how to make them do what he wanted, but he didn't really understand people at all. He always thought of them as somehow different, somehow beneath him, or rather that he was on a different, probably, but he was never that sure, elevated plane altogether. It wasn't that they were lesser people than him, but absolutely different, of that he was certain, and so he had never begun to see them in any way as his equals. Until he met Fiona that is - or rather until Fiona caught him. Because that was what had happened; he knew he was a good salesman, a subtle persuader, but Fiona had not succumbed to his charm, she hadn't been won over by his sales-pitch, by his diffident and unassuming persuasion, she was one of the very few who had walked away. She had not invested. He was almost sure that she would, he thought he had read the signs, he relaxed for a moment with the certain knowledge that she was hooked but then at the last minute she had declined. Well, you always lost a few. Instead she had turned the tables on him. She had, by appearing not to really care about him either and by seeming to cope very well without him, well and truly hooked and caught him. His very trick of letting people think he wasn't really bothered that much if they invested was, unbeknownst to him, used by Fiona to get her man. Or did he suspect, even as it was happening, as the hook caught in his gullet and he felt the slightest of tugs; did he know then that she had him on a line to her as secure as any fisherman's twine? Maybe he had in his own way really wanted it as much as her, but her seeming indifference, her lack of any obvious emotion had landed him safe and secure in her net.

The Philanthropist

It happened like this. They had dinner that first time and James, unpractised in dating simply chatted with her, uncertain if he should make a move, a pass, a suggestion that he fancied her even, or indeed if any such suggestion were even expected from him. He played it safe and waited for a signal from the enigmatic Fiona. And after the second dinner she went back to his flat and they made love. James somehow thought of this as a conquest, whereas Fiona would have slept with him on the very first date, or the third, or not at all if it turned out he wasn't that interested in sex. She might have been slightly disappointed, but though she enjoyed making love, it wasn't the thing that really attracted her to him. She was actually far more interested in probing him, in breaking his resistance down and even while sussing out his pad, discovering a little more about him. She too was intrigued, but in quite a different way. She had heard absolutely no rumours about him. Her girlfriends had no gossip about him at all. He was wealthy, successful and quite good-looking in a strange diffident way. But he was never seen after work, he didn't appear to drink, or not in the City watering holes they all frequented. He never overtly flirted with females either in the office or with potential clients. He was charming but he never gave any female the slightest hint that he might fancy them. She discreetly asked her girlfriends about him but drew a complete blank. More importantly they, none of them, had ever heard of any girlfriends he might have had. And yet she was sure he wasn't gay, she would have noticed that straight away. There were always small give-away signs and she was good at picking those up; no, she was sure he wasn't gay. And it was as if he simply disappeared after work, melted back into this vast city they all lived in, but it was more than just disappearing. He had no history except his work; nobody knew anything about him except the job he did so well. There were no family connections, no brothers or uncles in the City, no ex-colleagues, no school-friends - in fact nobody even knew exactly which school he had gone to. By this time the City was beginning to be invaded by self-made young traders, many who had flunked their secondary comprehensive educations, but James was obviously not one of those. No-one would ever assume he had anything but the best of educations. He carried himself confidently, he wore his clothes with a natural and understated elegance and he even spoke like one of the private school boys. And yet he was simply a blank page, an unknown quantity. And Fiona wanted to, indeed needed to, find out more about him.

They were politely chatting again on their second date and Fiona, feeling that maybe he would never make a move unless she did, feigned a slight yawn at exactly the right moment, just between dessert and coffee, one manicured hand covering her mouth. He smiled, looked at her and asked "You seem tired?"

"Not too tired. Let's get the bill and skip coffee, shall we?" And her hand reached out and touched his for the most fleeting of seconds. This was the first time their hands had met and it felt so right, so immediate that it almost took his breath away. He tried to look into her eyes but she had glanced away, scanning the busy Restaurant for the waiter and the bill.

When the waiter placed it discreetly in front of James and he was reaching into his jacket, she stole it away and handed it straight back to the waiter with her own American Express card. She must have had it palmed ready for this moment.

"Oh, I was going to get that." He protested.

"My treat. You can treat me another time. Let's go back to yours for coffee." She smiled knowingly and just as quickly, avoiding eye contact, glanced away, pushing her chair back and slipping on her cream bouclee jacket.

And she was fantastic in bed. Far better than the escort girls he still occasionally paid for. This time she was in control, and he didn't have to ask for anything. There was something incredibly sexy in a woman doing all the leading. Even with his first love he had been the one in control, pushing the boundaries, deciding what to do next. Fiona led, but by gentle suggestiveness, a languid letting him think he was making the running while all the while she was the only one in charge. She kept getting him almost to the edge and held him on the cusp of an orgasm for far longer than he was used to; teasing him almost to spilling over then relaxing and calming him down before leading him on even further. Even Joan, the older woman from Camden, hadn't been this good in bed. This was quite a new experience for James; he had never been in quite this situation before. And it was wonderful. He had always felt that to lose control would be his downfall, and here he was trying to second-guess her every move and then giving up and letting her lead him wherever she wanted to go. He felt so free, so alive, captivated and captive and rendered and surrendered, all at the same time. For years he had avoided any relationships, terrified to fall once more into a trap. He had paid for sex rather than risk getting caught again. He hadn't realised that buying sex was as much a trap as anything else, only a far more helpless and pathetic one. And after almost an hour in bed, when she had eventually let him come and as he lay there, eyes closed in the very moment, she leaned over and kissed him on the nose and said in an almost nonchalant way "I must be going, early start in the morning." It was as if they had just been having a nice cup of tea and a chat rather than exploring their bodies in the most electrifying and intimate way.

He was still recovering, exhausted, elated and not really aware of what she was saying. "Oh" he said, "What? I mean when?" and slumping his head back on the pillow, "I don't know what I mean." And he truly didn't. He had no ideas in his head at all other than wanting her to stay.

"Don't ring me." She called imperiously over her shoulder as she did her bra-clasp up and spun it round to pop her quite superb breasts into. "I'll ring *you*. Okay?" That 'Okay' was so serious that he didn't even begin to respond; he simply nodded his head as she zipped up her black silk dress and glanced at him over her shoulder.

And before he really knew it she was gone. It had all been so sudden, one minute he was coming gloriously at last after the most incredible sex he had ever experienced and then she was gone. He lay there still sweating, naked and hot on the bed and just as suddenly he felt very very cold and so terribly alone. More alone than he had ever felt before, it descended on him like an icy blanket. He was used to being alone, he liked being alone. He loved his own company, he avoided people, especially getting close to people, and yet now he felt almost devastatingly alone. "Fuck," he shouted out loud. "Fuck, fuck, fuck." And he thumped the pillow hard where minutes earlier she had laid her sweet auburn head. He knew he wanted her, more than anything he could remember. He just wanted her to return – he didn't want to spend another night alone.

A whole week went by before she rung him. He had been on the point of calling her several times, opening his filo-fax at her name, underlining it, posing question marks after it and then circling it in red, and wanting to, really wanting to - call her. But he was frightened of scaring her away, of offending her in some way. She had made it quite clear that she would call him. She had told him not to ring her with an authority in her voice which assured him that she meant it, and yet a week had almost passed and she hadn't called at all. Every time the phone rang he hoped it might be her, his heart leapt and he hesitated before picking it up and composing himself – but time after time it wasn't Fiona. And yet what would he say to her, how would he act? He wanted to see her again, he wanted to hold her, to be held, to be unfolded in her hands, disarmed in her arms - but he didn't know how to ask. He really had no idea what he would say, and then suddenly when he wasn't expecting it at all, when he was on the point of thinking she might never call him, she was there on the phone.

"Hi, it's me Fiona." She said so matter of fact, as if they were phoning each other every day.

"I know that, I recognise your voice" he said. "Where have you been?" he couldn't help himself.

"Did you miss me then?" she softly spoke, an almost shy conspiratorial whisper.

"A bit." He hesitated, "I mean it's not as if. I mean, I was surprised, that's all."

"Surprised? What? That I called?" with the hint of a playful laugh.

"No. I had hoped you might have called earlier, that's all. You told me not to call you, and I thought you might have called me sooner." He stupidly explained just that bit too much.

"Wow. A man who does what he has been told; I'd better not let go of you in a hurry." And she laughed, and he caught the infectiousness and started to laugh too.

"Why, were you thinking of letting me go?" he said "I was rather hoping we might …"

"Have another dinner? Or what?" And he could almost see her smiling at the other end of the phone, that funny little half-smile of hers. Not really a smile at all but a smile as if she was smiling for his eyes only, a secret smile just between the two of them.

"Yes. Dinner would be lovely, and actually we never got to having coffee last time. I will make sure I have some coffee ready next time."

"Actually I'm not that blown away by coffee, it tends to make me sleep rather than keep me awake. But yes, let's do it again. Soon."

"Tonight?" he said just a bit too quickly.

"If you are not too busy? I know how your clients keep you tied to your work, mustn't let another investment slip away again." She was fencing with him again, tempting him to defy her.

"And why on earth would you think that might be the case. I would happily cancel anyone for dinner again with you. You must be aware of that." Suddenly serious with almost a catch in his voice he let her know how much he wanted her.

And then she knew she had caught him. She felt the pull on the line, no need to reel him in just yet.

And so they started a glorious long hot summer of twice weekly dinner and sex. Or sometimes it was sex followed by a late dinner, or sex and an Indian takeaway eaten cross-legged in bed, the rice and curry sauce spilling out of the foil containers and staining the bed-sheets a yellowy-brown which despite several washes never quite faded. Sometime they went to his Marylebone flat, and sometimes to hers in Islington. But she was never pushy, she didn't invade his space. She left nothing of herself behind, no clothes, no make-up; even keeping her toothbrush wrapped in cling-film in her handbag. She left their weekends free. She also asked that they not phone each other daily, "Let's not be in each other's pockets; let's be grown-up about this, shall we?" And there were nights he desperately wanted to, needed to call her, just to hear her voice but he didn't. It was clear that she had laid down the ground rules and he was careful not to tread anywhere near them. She never called him either, though he wished she would have, if only just once. Again that ambivalence nagging at him, the niggling toothache that won't go away – does she feel anything like the way I feel about her?

One night after making love in her Islington flat, just off the Liverpool road, he asked her if he could see her over a weekend, maybe they could go for a run in the country, stay at a hotel somewhere. It did cross his mind that she might have another lover at the weekend (or in his panic – a husband and kids, she staying up in town the working week) but he tried to push those thoughts away. Jealousy was a spectre he had no desire to invite to this particularly delicious feast. The weekends now were his desert, stretching on and on, so many hours to fill, no work to mop up the days, so much sand trickling slowly through the hourglass. Time on his own used to be his secret pleasure, now he wandered around his luxury flat, picking up some latest gadget and rapidly discarding it, too bored to read a book or watch television and even his music began to pall. He had heard it all before.

"Now you're beginning to get a bit serious, aren't you James? I'm not sure if either of us wants this to become serious." She said, knowing that was exactly what he wanted.

"Well it only need be as serious as we need it to be, needn't it? If that makes any sense, or if that sentence is even English." He laughed at his own ineptitude.

"Okay, but are you ready for this?" she spoke quietly, barely a whisper, as she changed the mood from light to serious in an instant.

"What do you mean, ready? We've been fucking like horses all summer. I would just like to spend a weekend with you." He paused but she didn't respond. "Occasionally, not every or even most weekends; I'm not suggesting moving in with you." He looked around her smart flat, with the carefully chosen discreet Miro reproductions and modern but functional furniture and would have actually been quite happy moving in with her.

"I know. But so far this has been extremely uncommitted. On both our parts - I thought you preferred it that way." Her fingers wove patterns in his chest hairs as she refused to look into his eyes.

"I wouldn't exactly say that. You've made me very happy, if you want to know."

"And I don't want to make you unhappy. I don't want to spoil it. Getting too serious has a nasty habit of spoiling things, don't you find?" as she kissed one small red nipple and then the other.

"Well, if you like I promise not to fall in love with you." She sat up and looked directly at him. "I won't say ever, but at least for the next week or two. Will that do?" he asked, opening his hands out to her, when it was really his heart he was holding out.

"Come over here and let me test that theory out." And she held his hands shut and pulled him on top of her.

"To the hilt?" he asked.

"Oh, absolutely to the hilt. No point in half-doing things," as they sealed their new arrangement in the traditional manner.

By the Autumn they were seeing each other most weekends. She had asked about his family and he told her an evasive half-truth. He hadn't seen them in years, and to be honest he didn't want to see them again. She knew this was some sort of a lie, but if he didn't want to tell her that was up to him, wasn't it. One night as they lay sated in his bed she asked if he would be prepared to see her parents; she sort-of saw them herself three or four times a year, it was expected that she spend Christmas and their birthdays at home at the very least. He asked her how she would explain his presence.

"I am allowed boyfriends you know. I am thirty-seven years old. I think they might excuse me this once, don't you think?"

"Yes, but how many boyfriends have you taken back before? And what sort of scrutiny were they put under? 'And exactly what are your intentions towards my daughter, young man?'" he intoned in a deep fatherly tone. "That sort of thing." He asked, suddenly a bit nervous, he hadn't once really considered any family she might have.

"Actually, I have been engaged before," she confessed, without apologising. "Twice, if you need to know, but no more details will be forthcoming. And my parents, bless them, have sort of given up on me ever settling down with anyone." She looked down on him as she straddled him on the bed, her sex inches from his face. "Besides we made a pact, didn't we? What went on before is not a subject for conversation." A finger to his lips "I don't want to know about your exes, and you may not ask, though like all men you are dying to know, about those who may have gone before you."

"Agreed. And for the record I would much rather not know." As he nibbled at her pendant breasts, "Blissful ignorance remains my preferred state in relation to your past. I like to imagine you have just arrived, pre-packaged and perfect in the post, with no previous owners."

"I am not sure I can be so placid, and actually I know very little about you. I couldn't give a fuck about your past partners, but it would be nice to know just exactly who you are, Mister James Pilkington?" as she pulled away from him slightly.

"I am exactly what you see. No mystery, no strange perverted past life." He frowned and continued. "If you must know I left home, Suffolk, at eighteen. Ran away actually; or more mundanely, boarded a train to London without telling anyone beforehand. I was all set to go to University, which I assume you did go to, when I just upped sticks and came to London. I felt it was all too easy, too ordained from above; maybe I wanted to prove something to myself. Who knows, we are all confused at eighteen. Almost on a whim you might say. I made a vow to myself that I wouldn't contact my parents, and I am an only child, until I had made something of my life. That took quite a few years longer than I expected, and by that time I had sort of decided not to. It had been too long already without speaking and it all seemed a bit pointless; why rake up the past. I chickened out and avoided the inevitable recriminations. It all seems such a long time ago now; to be honest I hardly think about them anymore. It is as if I was a totally different person then, I wouldn't recognise me myself now." He fluently re-invented his back-story, how easy it was when you got started.

The beginnings of his reviving erection had subsided and she lay down next to him and said, "Haven't you ever felt guilty about leaving home? I mean they are probably devastated that you went away like that. Aren't you at least curious about them?"

"I know, but strangely I am not that curious. I suppose I have put them out of my mind, they have their own lives to lead. But sometimes I have thought about it, and maybe I should have. Looking at it from the outside, of course I should have contacted them, but the longer you leave things the harder it becomes to put them right. And besides what right do I have now to go back and thrust myself into their lives. They've gotten used to me not being there a long time ago. They are probably settled into old-age by now; they had me late in life anyway. And what worries me most is – yes, I could go back, I expect they're still in the same house in the same little town, but what if it didn't work out? What if there were recriminations, questions, accusations and bitterness? What then? Better maybe to just leave things as they are. Do you think I am callous?" he looked into her hazel-flecked eyes. This was the closest to any truth he had ever told anyone and he was hoping he hadn't said too much, even though it was far from honesty.

"I wouldn't exactly say callous. Unfeeling, selfish, cowardly certainly, and uncaring; yes – but not callous. But I can't make you see them, can I?" she sat up, glancing at the clock, and began picking her clothes from the floor. "Anyway it isn't up to me at all. I decided; when we started this, to keep it light. I am not here to criticise you, especially about stuff before I knew you. I don't want to fuck it up and I don't want you to fuck it up either. I think we are both pretty selfish people who find it difficult to share. I was an only child too and I never learnt to share. My parents gave me everything I ever asked for and I don't like people saying no to me. I have had, well let's just say, quite a few relationships, and I have managed singlehandedly to fuck them all up; I really need no help on that front at all." She leaned over and kissed him briefly on the nose, "Just be there for me. When I need someone, be there for me. That's all I will ever ask of you. None of that love you forever and ever bollocks, just be there for me."

But of course that was not all she ever asked of him. It never is, is it? After a year they were practically living together, mostly at his Marylebone flat, but she was careful not to move too many of her things in, just the clothes she needed for a day or two, a toothbrush, a razor and shampoo; his bathroom remained Spartan and uncluttered. She bought a portable TV to watch in the bedroom, and a deluxe pair of headphones for him to listen to his music without disturbing either of them. James liked the arrangement, she was there with him but his routine hadn't been changed completely. She left him alone for hours at a time, she didn't bring her work problems home with her, and she cooked a mean Jalfrezi. One day she looked up from her magazine and suggested that maybe she should sell her flat; she was hardly using it really.

"Not a bad idea, it must be worth a fortune now. Who would have thought Islington would ever be *the* place to live. It certainly wasn't when I came to London twenty odd years ago. It really was a shithole back then," he said, not realising at all what she meant. "This place, Marylebone, is expensive, but it was when I bought the place, you must have bought your flat for next to nothing."

"Yes, I've done very well thank-you." She replied and realising she would have to enlighten him (why do men never understand what we are trying to tell them) she continued, "But what I mean is, maybe we should buy somewhere together. Somewhere bigger, you could have your own music room, your own bedroom if you like; we needn't be in each other's hair all the time."

"Buy somewhere together? Like a proper couple you mean? And I would presumably sell this place too." He had never thought this moment might arrive; Fiona had always seemed quite ambivalent about their relationship. "Wouldn't that be rather serious? I thought you wanted to keep it light?"

"I do. And I think I am doing just that. We don't have to be like other couples, we can be together because we want to be." And then more seriously, "You do want to be with me, don't you?"

"Yes. And I imagine I might be mildly upset for a day or two if it ended. I rather like having you around. You may have noticed that occasionally," he joked. "Seriously though, are you proposing we become a real couple?" He held her hand and looked into her eyes, trying to read what she was really thinking (it was so hard sometimes to know).

"If you like. On the surface at least. It makes sense financially too, and if it didn't work out, so what? We could sell whatever we buy together and go our separate ways. I'm not actually proposing marriage you know." And she looked at him, the intensity of her gaze belying her words, "I like being around you, we get on okay. No, we get on better than okay. But this is still your place, or if we are at mine it is my place. I think we might like having *our* place, that's all."

"Let's think about it. Silly to rush into anything." He said calmly, trying to appear as nonchalant as Fiona while he was secretly elated at the prospect.

"Sure, no problem." And she returned to her magazine, slowly turning the pages but not reading a word.

Kensington

A year later and they moved into their really rather large apartment in Kensington. Kensington is probably the poshest district of all in London but carries with it an impersonal air; as if it has seen it all before, riches and fame impress it not at all. Their apartment was in a large red-brick Edwardian block with a large marble foyer, and a uniformed concierge they never used; it had three large bedrooms, two en-suite and two decent sized sitting rooms. The only room they would really have to share was the kitchen, and he hardly ever used his in Marylebone. They had quite a bit of money left from the transactions and bought new beds and sofa's and left most of their old stuff behind. He moved his quite large record and growing CD collection with him, and indulged in an even more expensive hi-fi set-up. In some ways nothing changed that much, they both had their own flats, just under one roof. They tended to have sex in his room, Fiona deciding when. It was most nights anyway, so James never felt neglected, but she didn't like staying the night. She would wait until he fell into that semi-exhausted slumber after coming, and would slide out of his arms and into the splendid comfort of her own cool sheets. He sometimes woke in the middle of the night and was never sure if he was quietly happy or a little bit sad that she was no longer there beside him. At least she was in the same flat, just across the hall; he didn't have to lay there as he heard her crunching the gears of her Merc as she returned to her Islington pad.

Work days they had their routine of shaving and showering and breakfast on the run. They both liked starting early and would leave the apartment by seven. Fiona was careful to make every weekend some sort of an event. They often flew off somewhere; Paris, Rome or Amsterdam, or his favourite city - Barcelona. Staying in unassuming but quietly expensive small hotels, twin rooms please, they enjoyed a luxury lifestyle without ever getting into any sort of debt. They were both very well-paid and bonuses seemed to tumble their way with increasing regularity. They both kept their own money, but had a joint account to cover the apartment costs. They had an arrangement that on these weekend jaunts they would alternate their expenditure, one time James would pay for everything and the next it would be Fiona's turn. James had a habit of trying to top Fiona's efforts but it never bothered her, she seemed oblivious to his financial generosity.

So, a perfect arrangement. Or was it? Isn't it always the case that as Joni sang 'you never know what you got 'til it's gone'? In their own ways both were a bit unhappy, though on the surface it was so perfect, no ripple to disturb the calmest of ponds. They always smiled when they met in the evenings and were polite, civilised despite any private misgivings. They never argued, they never complained. They were professional people after all, and above all that jealousy and fractiousness they saw in so many couples. The trouble was James was never sure if she loved him, or indeed what, if anything, she really felt for him. He knew that he loved her; he had never met anyone quite like her. He was besotted in his own silent way, though careful not to show it too much, it was all just a bit too good to be true. He felt as if he was some naughty schoolboy, allowed on sufferance to remain in the classroom, but always on his guard, he could be caught, found out and might be expelled at any moment. So, he assumed an air of mild indifference, as if he were scared to let her know just how much he adored her, but at times he was deeply worried that she was just too good for him, he was an imposter after all, and sooner or later she would come to that conclusion too. Things couldn't simply remain this un-committed for this long, could they? And there was such an air of 'couldn't care less' about Fiona that he was secretly scared that it might all end, some whim might take her fancy and she would simply choose to end it, or worse - just not be there when he came home one day. She was so insistent on it all being light and breezy that sometimes he felt there was nothing to even hold on to. Even her scent seemed to dissipate the moment she was gone. Her habit of slipping away after sex began to rankle. He would have loved to roll over in the night and bump into her, instead of this vast and empty king-size bed. He always felt that she might just up and leave at any time, instead of leaving for her own bed she might quietly dress and walk right out the door; and the thought, the very possibility, began to terrify him. Sometimes he even woke in the early hours and would stand silently at her door, watching her sleep, counting her breaths, amazed by her beauty even asleep. Or maybe he was just checking that she was still there.

Despite his success, at work and even here with Fiona, he knew he was an imposter, an interloper, a cuckoo who had successfully deposited himself into a very comfy nest. The money was his alright, and he still liked to keep his spreadsheets up to date, checking and rechecking the various bank statements, moving money around to get a slightly better interest rate. He never actually invested in his own company, even though the return would have been better. He just felt that somehow he didn't deserve all of this, the luxury flat, the electronic toys, the flights, the checking-in to hotels. It all seemed as if it should be happening to someone else (and in a way it was, of course) and not to him. It wasn't that he felt guilty so much as that it was all temporary, that it might all be snatched away from him, that he might wake up one morning back on the streets behind Waterloo with nothing but dreams and a filthy old sleeping bag for home. Or a knock on the door one evening might herald in a Policeman addressing him by his real, his almost forgotten name. In fact maybe this whole existence was just a dream he was having, one day he would wake up and have to admit who he really was. But who was that person, certainly nobody he recognised now at all. He didn't even know himself anymore - maybe he had never known who he was. Perhaps this unknowingness, even of his own self, had enabled him to transfer himself so easily into other lives, other identities. But those dreams of being good, of doing something positive in the world had never gone away. That had been some sort of constant idea, often pushed back but forcing itself to the surface of his late-night thoughts. And even now, when by almost everyone's standards he must be happy the thought still worried him; what good was he possibly doing in this world? He hated politics, he knew that was the biggest game of all, there was no way they would ever really change anything. But did he really want to change things anyway? Where had all those teenage ideas gone? Or had they? One part of him still harboured some idealistic dream of doing something important with his life; but he was never quite sure how. This wealth for wealth sake was no end in itself surely; it was just perpetuating the system. The game was still being played, even if he knew it was a game and was better at the game than most it still remained a game. There had to be something more. Surely, this wasn't it, was it?

Fiona was also unhappy, though far more careful to hide it. Except to herself. She had pursued him, she had ensnared him, and now that she had him she still felt as if she didn't really know what she had. Or actually if she really wanted him now that he was safely in her grasp. He was such an unknowable person, despite her occasional probing into his past she still knew very little about him. She had been careful in not scaring this one away; she had done that many times before. But what did she really want from him? The sex was good, but then sex was almost always good. She made sure of that, she was always subtly in control. Even if she let him think he was the conductor the baton was firmly in her hands, she knew exactly when to bring in the gentle swell of the violins and when to let the timpani roar. And yet sometimes even sex bored her. She would be laying there thinking 'what the hell am I doing' while he was pounding in to her. 'What the hell am I doing with my life, wasting my time on this nonsense? Oh come on Fiona, concentrate – he's getting near to the end soon, not long now and you can sleep. But what is it I really want from this man?" The thoughts pounding into her brain at the same time as her body was being pummelled. And none of it was resolved; no amount of pounding could shift the big issue she was facing.

What did she really want? That was the question pounding in her mind, and the answer was always the same. It had been there since she was in her twenties and no amount of external pounding had dislodged it an inch. Despite all her coolness, her success at work, her calm nonchalant exterior; inside she was just the same as other women. She wanted a child. No, she assured herself, it was not just a question of wanting – she needed a child. A child of her own, a girl ideally, but if it were a boy that would suffice; just one child, not children. Definitely not children, just one sweet child of her own would make her life complete. All the success, all the exams passed; the plaudits at work, the money she had made; all of this meant nothing compared to the still un-conceived child that resided so real and breathing and smiling in her mind. But not with just anyone; it had to be the right man, the right genes. There had to be something about him to make her sure he would be the perfect father of her child - and with James she just wasn't sure. He was closer than any before, but there was this nagging doubt. What was it about him that she was unsure of; but that was precisely what she was didn't know. Although she had refused his financial investment she had invested three years now of her precious life on him, it was time she had some return for all that hard work.

Getting pregnant was the easiest thing in the world, surely. Avoiding it was harder. But she desperately wanted this child of her own. She felt that a child would complete her, make her whole. She believed that a child would give her selfish little life some meaning. She needed security, the security of wealth, a good job and the right father for her child. But none of that security meant a thing without that very child to place in the empty cot she always imagined beside her bed. Sometimes dreaming or on waking her hand would reach out for the crib and rock thin and desolate air.

But she was still unsure of James. In some ways she barely knew him, she had always made sure to leave him unthreatened, to let him feel that she was there just for him and she didn't know how to even begin to talk about a child. They had barely talked about their future; it was always left open, an unsigned contract sitting in the bureau drawer. But not talking about the future, while a strategy to keep him from bolting, meant there was a void at the heart of their relationship. And while she imagined that James might be satisfied with this unthreatening open-ended affair, she definitely was not. She wanted a child and ideally she wanted him to be the father, it was just that talking about it seemed so impossible.

And she was getting older. Every day she looked in the mirror, and despite the good bone structure (thank you Mum) she couldn't help seeing the truth, that she was getting older. Those eyelids were losing elasticity and beginning to droop, her lips were a touch thinner and her neck despite the most expensive creams money could buy had the very whisper of scraggy-ness about it. She was almost forty; soon she would be too old. So she simply decided not to mention it. If it was an impossible subject to raise maybe not raising it at all was the solution. She smiled sweetly as if nothing was bothering her, no ripples must disturb the perfect placid pond, especially if turbulence beneath the water was to be disguised and never to be seen.

She suddenly stopped taking the pill. One day while popping the pill out of the plastic holster she decided not to load the gun but to get rid of all the bullets; she slipped the pack into the trash. She carried on applying her make-up, taking extra care with her new eye-liner and not even giving the packet of pills in the bin another glance. Satisfied with her eye make-up application she turned back and slipped a sly wink at her own beautiful image. She wouldn't tell James, she barely acknowledged it to herself. It wasn't as if stopping taking the pill was a decision to get pregnant in itself, was it? She just decided to wait and see what happened. She had never been pregnant; she had no idea if she could even conceive. What if she were one of those women who simply couldn't get pregnant? Barren, they used to be called. Surely 'barren' was the loneliest word in the dictionary. And if she did fall, if her body responded to her heart's innermost desire, why then that would be a bridge she would just have to cross, there would be no turning back, it would be fate, kismet really. It would be too late by then, if he wasn't prepared to stay with her so be it. She would much rather go through this with him than alone, but if alone then that would be okay too. Ready to leave she returned to the mirror and as she applied her lip-gloss she pursed those red lips and mewed a little kiss to the one person she really loved.

As it happened it didn't take that long. Four months in and she was late. Just three days but she knew. She didn't say anything. Of course it could just be a false alarm. Or she might miss-carry; she was almost forty after all. No, she decided to just wait a bit longer, and then a few weeks more, and then when one more period had failed to materialise she knew she had to see her doctor. She decided she would tell James when it was confirmed. And it was. I mean, what else could it have been Fiona? The doctor congratulated her with the slightest hint of hesitation.

"Oh, it's okay I am in a permanent relationship."

"Well, I am sure your partner and you will both be delighted at the news."

"Oh yes. We've been trying for ages really, but with my age and all we weren't sure if we had left it too late." She dissembled.

"You are a very fit and healthy woman, there should be no complications. I will pass on your notes to our midwife who will contact you shortly. Good luck."

She was floating on air as she walked home, each step felt like walking on cushions. She hardly gave a thought as to how James would take it; her head was full of pretty little dresses, fluffy teddies and a little girl smiling up at her. He came in soon after her and asked what was for dinner.

"Ah, I thought we might eat out tonight." She said.

"Oh, okay. Any particular reason?"

"Yes. I have something to tell you." A slight note of seriousness creeping into her voice.

"Nothing dreadful I hope" he joked (but you never knew).

"No, on the contrary, something wonderful. I wanted to tell you over dinner but actually I can't wait." It was now or never she thought and just blurted it out. "I've just come back from my Doctor's. James, I'm pregnant."

"Pregnant? Are you sure? I mean, how did that happen? No, I know how it happened. I didn't mean that, I meant … I just thought you were on the pill." Perplexed, he had never expected this, not once. "I never realised you wanted a child. Why didn't you say? Why didn't we discuss it?"

And careful to avoid an argument (they didn't do arguments), she ignored his questioning her motives and joked about the mechanics. Always stick to the mechanics, not the motive – that was the best advice her boss in chambers had given her. It worked in law and she prayed it would work now.

"I don't know how it happened either. It does apparently, sometimes. Nothing is a hundred percent. And we have been doing it rather a lot. Aren't you happy for me? For both of us?" her beaming smile told him just how delighted she was.

And how could he answer that one without betrayal? Even hesitation might infer betrayal; he played for time.

"Well I have to think about it, you know. It's such a surprise. Last thing I ever expected, especially as you never seemed the 'mumsy' type." And as the reality coalesced into his mind he realised it was the glue to fix the final piece of the puzzle firmly into place. "But in a funny way I am delighted. Yes, of course I am. And you Fi? You seem happy too. I assume that this is what you want too."

"Yes, it is. Of course I was as surprised as you, but ever since I have known I have realised it was meant to be." And pulling him to her she smothered his face with kisses. "And yes, I am ecstatically happy too. I feel it was somehow meant to happen, an affirmation of the last few years. Isn't it wonderful."

"I suppose it means we will have to become a proper couple, instead of playing at it like we have been." He replied, kissing her back and holding her tight.

"What do you mean 'playing at it'? I wasn't playing at anything." She pulled back a bit and looked right into his eyes. "I have deliberately tried to make you happy in every possible way, and I just knew you didn't want cosy domesticity. James, you have had your cake and eaten it too in a way; and wiped your grubby little finger round the plate to pick up all the crumbs as well, you lucky man. It has been quite an achievement really; we weren't like other couples, always in each other's hair, always bickering or despising each other. We both needed our own space, but I think we also needed each other too. Deep down I think we needed each other, don't you?"

"God, I needed you Fiona, I can tell you that. I might as well say it, though you must have known. I love you. I really love you." He smiled down at her. "It's just that sometimes I wasn't sure how you felt about me. It was as if that wasn't a discussion we were ever allowed to have." She leaned up to kiss him. "But this changes everything doesn't it? There's no just walking away if we don't like it anymore. Not that I have ever had any intention of walking away at all."

"You can if you want. I mean, this was never in the contract was it; not even in the small print which no-one ever reads." She paused a moment to make sure, and then. "*Do* you love me James? Or are you just saying that because I am pregnant?"

"Yes, I think so. No, I know so. I have always loved you. I've always known it, and so do you, you must have known how I loved you. Look, I had a bad relationship when I first came to London. Bad? No it was wonderful in a way, but we were far too young and I was stupid. And, well it ended badly, and I swore I would never fall in love again. I concentrated on making money, on becoming successful and I avoided relationships. I had a few one-night things, but I always ran away as soon as it got a bit heavy, you know. And I thought I had it sussed. I would never need a woman; I would never lose my heart again. And then I met you, and well – you must have known, I worship you."

"Oh how sweet, and you never told me." She coyly replied.

"That's because I sort of felt I wasn't allowed to." He replied, serious to her levity. "I could never quite bring myself to believe you might be real, that you would stay. You once said "none of that lovey-dovey forever and ever bollocks" and I thought you meant it."

"Oh I did. At first. But as time has gone on I have learnt to trust you. And in my own funny way I do love you Mr. Unknowable James Pilkington. Will you be the father of my child?"

"It seems, lawyer that you are, that you have already decided that. But yes, as you are asking I would love to be the father of your child. Can we start trying tonight?"

"Oh yes, and I promise to let you come inside me too."

"Hmmm, now that might be interesting, I suppose we could try that for a change." He laughingly suggested. "Actually, far more important - I am fucking starving. I think you mentioned eating out a while ago, get your coat on missus and follow me."

And that was how easy it was. Fiona had been, well, not exactly dreading telling him, but certainly wary. Unsure. She was that little bit nervous of his reaction. One part of her was aware she could handle it, turn his reaction around; manipulate him even, into agreement. But there was maybe a tenth of her mind that was uncertain. What if he just walked out, or lashed out at her even? Screamed his anger at her or accused her of deliberately getting pregnant. In a way she couldn't blame him, and she had already decided that even if he broke it off there and then she would go it alone. Nothing and nobody would stop her having this baby now that at last she was actually pregnant.

And James, though at first surprised was delighted too. It meant, or he assumed it meant that now he had her. That constant fear he had was evaporating fast. She wouldn't leave him now that she was going to be a mother. Maybe this had been her way of keeping him too, but surely she knew he would never leave her. Strangely he had never really thought about being a father himself. When he was younger, in his teens, he was absolutely sure he wouldn't be trapped by wife and kids, that mediocre life that everyone else lived. He was different, he was cleverer than that. There was no way he would fall into that trap. Then he had slipped, taken his eye off the ball, allowed himself to fall in love. With all the stupidity of blind love he had gotten that girl pregnant, and even then he had tried to play the game. Well, it had ended with him deserting her; walking away into the rainy night, walking away from everything he loved. Losing it all, but finding a way out of the trap despite that. He thought kids were for losers, for those with no imagination to look for something else to do with their lives. But what had he done really that was so much cleverer? Made a lot of money by playing the game a bit smarter than most - that was all. There was no more 'purpose in his life' than all those trapped in the game. What had he achieved all those years alone in his flat in Marylebone, sitting there replaying the records of his youth and waiting for the escort girl's knock on the door. Wasn't he just as trapped as the rest of them? And then he had met Fiona, and even though he knew and saw that it was another trap he couldn't stop himself from falling into it. Maybe he just thought, why not? One trap is much like another, isn't it? But no, this trap had been wonderful. Trap that it might have been it was soft and warm and gorgeously wonderful. And now that ultimate trap of all was staring him in the face too.

He was going to become a father. He, the one who thought that having kids was for losers; he was going to be a father. But if that was the price to keep Fiona then okay, if that was the terms of the contract, he would sign up. He had of course signed up years ago, and though she was right and he had neglected to read the small print; well, what did it matter - he had Fiona now. He didn't for one moment believe that she had accidentally gotten herself pregnant. She was an intelligent woman, maybe the most intelligent one he had ever met. She had stopped taking the pill. Absolutely, for certain. This child was no accident. But if she wanted to maintain the fiction, okay he would go along with that. She had so obviously planned the whole thing, especially as she hadn't said a word until she was almost three month's gone. Did she think he was stupid? Of course not. She must know that he saw through it all too, but actually none of that mattered. It suited them both not to delve too far into exactly how she got pregnant. She may have thought that she had trapped him, ensnared him in a way. But actually he now had her just as surely as she had him. She was caught and netted down too, no more lepidopteron flitting around, acting as if she might up and leave at any moment. She was pinned down now, and even though her body was pupating and a new life-form about to emerge she was undoubtedly his now too, the brightest specimen he had ever seen.

But he was about to make the biggest mistake of his life. He thought he had her, at last, within his grasp. But Fiona, sweet butterfly that she was, was merely resting, taking her time, nurturing her child until they were both old enough to survive without him. And he couldn't say he hadn't been warned. "None of that forever and ever bollocks," she had laughingly said. He just never realised that she had meant it.

Buckinghamshire

They were married in the 16th Century church in the pretty Buckinghamshire village Fiona had been born into and where her successful stockbroker father and devoted mother had lived ever since. Even though Fiona was almost seven months pregnant and wore a Regency-style (flowing from the bust) off-white dress covered in pearls and lace, which had cost a fortune, her father was so proud; he was nearly eighty and was beginning to despair that his only child would ever settle down and marry; her mother was more circumspect and sighed in quiet and wondered what on earth the world was coming to, she was far more relieved than proud. But she was determined to keep her head up; the guests might all know that Fiona was pregnant, the dress left little to the imagination after all, but the important thing was that nobody actually mentioned it. Not openly anyway, think what you like in private but please don't say anything; besides this was 1992 for heaven's sake, times had moved on. Who really cared, well she did of course, but Fiona was happy at last, they were a successful couple - that was all that really mattered. And best of all she was moving back to Buckinghamshire, her roots. No more gallivantin' up in London; oh she had done well, nobody could deny that; a brilliant lawyer apparently, but now she was coming home and she was going to be a mother, time to settle down at last.

They honeymooned in Thailand, and Fiona was uncomfortable on the plane, the seat belt straining against her tummy. She was uncomfortable on the beach, with her lacy sarong only partially covering her lump. She was uncomfortable even back in their luxury air-conned hotel; whichever way she tried to sleep she was uncomfortable alongside James in this double bed; she had requested a twin, but the hotel was full so they settled for a double. In the end James slept badly on the guest sofa, all four foot six of it, with his legs hung over the end and almost touching the floor, and still Fiona was uncomfortable. Hot and uncomfortable, she wasn't really enjoying being pregnant at all and maybe Thailand had been a mistake. But she smiled and smiled, after all she only had herself to blame. Actually she was restless more than uncomfortable, because she couldn't wait to get back and start packing up the flat. The honeymoon had been James's idea, to get away from England for a week, clear their heads before the move. It had made perfect sense to move out of London; it was all very well if you were a young childless couple but not exactly the best place to raise a family. (And besides, they had made a fortune on the Kensington apartment, house prices were surging in London yet again.) In Buckinghamshire she would have her mother and her cousins, and all her old friends, mostly with children in their teens admittedly, but all on hand to help out if needed.

James hadn't even argued with her, come to think of it he had never argued with her – why was that? He reasoned that if that was what she wanted, okay he would go along with it. Besides he was getting tired of London too. That maelstrom, all that rush and bustle, that anonymity he had craved as a young man was palling. He had traded in anonymity for respectability a long time ago. He never for a moment thought about returning to his home-town in Suffolk, there was nothing for him there and Fiona's little Buckinghamshire village was chocolate-box pretty, he couldn't argue with that. So why not, he had gone along with everything – one more move wouldn't really hurt. There had been an awkward moment about his parents, James insisted they couldn't possibly be invited to the wedding (how would he ever explain his new name, let alone the years of absence) so Fiona reluctantly agreed to simply say they had both died of cancer a couple of years back. So sad, everyone muttered. And then instantly forgot about it, as you do. So James was hijacked, lock stock and double-barrelled Purdey shotgun, and moved out of the city to England's green and pleasant rural idyll.

And he went along with it all, no arguments, no regrets and actually very little real thought. If this was the price Fiona was exacting - if this was what had to be done to have her completely - okay he was willing to pay. This had so obviously been planned by Fiona from the start; getting herself pregnant the perfect way to hook him. Even James had to admit that if she had ever suggested having a child or moving back to her home village he would have instinctively hated the idea, and maybe he would have lost her in the process. This way they both got what they wanted, Fiona her child and he Fiona, and no-one got hurt.

And so just before the baby girl Eleanor was born they moved from noisy Kensington to one of Buckinghamshire's more wealthy and secluded villages, where the hum of Range Rovers dropping wee ones off at the kinder-garden was the only sound you heard above the twittering of birdsong in the morning. James drove his brand new Audi TT to the small railway station and commuted into London every morning. Someone had to keep earning a wage after all; the rather-too-large Buckinghamshire house had used up all the Kensington money and swallowed most of their savings too. At first he rather liked this daily journey, along with all the other business suits, broadsheet newspapers meticulously folded into a quarter, gold cuff-links flashing as they completed the cryptic crossword, polite conversation as the tiny train chugged its merry little way into Marylebone station. But there were moments when he too wondered exactly what on earth he was doing here. These weren't his people; he had nothing in common with these middle class 'oiks'. But then he had nothing in common with anyone. He never had. He had always been a loner; he had always felt outside of whatever was going on. A watcher, never really participating, always too self-conscious of his difference, he was the outsider perpetually looking in on others. He had never felt at one with his classmates or any of the people he ended up working with either. He had always acted the part, the hippy second-hand record stall-holder, the slick car dealer, the financial director and the City investment salesman. Always the actor and never the man he was portraying. Inside he knew he was a loner, and no more alone in these commuter trains than tramping the streets of Waterloo in the cold and the rain. He had been a loner at school, he had actually been a loner in his own family; a thinker of thoughts; subversive and manipulative - but always a loner. And now he in his turn was being manipulated, turned into something he almost certainly never was or had never aspired to be. And deep inside he knew he would always be an outsider, a loner; except maybe in the arms of Fiona. Here he could lose himself completely; he could forget himself and just be; no false name, no pretending at school, no acting the part anymore, no being someone he wasn't. Here he could just be. Closer to his real self than any time before, and yet still a part of him aware, watching, observing as he tried to lose himself completely, concentrating on the moment.

So, he gritted his teeth and rolled up his Daily Telegraph, unread mostly, and smiled and played the game, and all for the love of Fiona. Through it all, the daily charade, the boring dinner parties they felt obliged to attend, the stuffy Sundays spent with her parents; always his thoughts returned time and again to the prize he had won. Fiona was his now. In commerce there is always a price to pay; it was simply a matter of weighing up the pros and cons. And the move to Buckinghamshire, the giving up of his independence, the whole marriage shebang and even little Eleanor – they were the price he had to pay for the safety, the security, the winning of and the constant love of Fiona.

And Eleanor too. He had barely thought of the child in all of this. The child had been the price to pay, part of the contract, but he had almost neglected the fact that he would now be a father. And he hadn't begun to realise how he would fall in love with that child too. In a different and yet possibly deeper way than he loved Fiona herself. He would love this child unconditionally; almost instantly from the very moment of her birth he would love her. And not for what she might give him, but actually for what he might give her. They called her Eleanor, or rather Fiona did. He liked the name; it seemed perfect, even if he hadn't even really thought what sex he might prefer. Unlike most men he wasn't interested in sport at all and had no illusions of teaching a boy to play football or cricket, so when the midwife said (just after the head was out and Fiona was still digging her nails into his palm and panting like a dog as, slippery and purple, she emerged into the world) "It's a girl. A darling little girl" he was suddenly ecstatic. A girl. Of course it was a girl. What else could it have possibly been? For the third time in his life he fell in love. So the Philanthropist was maybe not that different from the rest of us, after all. How perfect life was, as he walked out of the Maternity ward that bright April morning he thought he must truly be the luckiest man alive. But strangely at this moment he never paused for a moment to consider his own parents and how unconditionally they too may have once loved him, and how he had returned that love in so uncaring a manner. So it goes.

It started with little niggles, comments muttered almost under her breath. Just loud enough for him to catch the fact that she was unhappy, but quiet enough to be ignored if he so chose. Mostly he decided not to say anything; he smiled and patted her knee, tried to reassure her, it would be okay, he understood how tedious this being a mother could be. She complained mostly of tiredness, and though he was tired too he tried to be sympathetic. Eleanor woke almost every two hours and demanded attention, especially in the middle of the night. It felt as if he had only just got back to sleep when that little face with the big cry started up again. He was falling asleep on the train both ways, and even caught himself nodding off at work between meetings. But Fiona said it was getting her down. She insisted that Eleanor was worse during the day, hardly sleeping at all, she said. At least you could escape her at work she sniped. It was hardly escaping he protested. But not too loudly, after all arguments were never their style. He agreed that they should get a nanny; they could afford it because Fiona was still being paid for a few more months, besides they still had some savings left and no mortgage. And so the part-time nanny was hired and settled into the top floor bedroom where she looked after, fed and changed the baby at night, leaving at eight each morning. And though now at last they were getting a full night's sleep Fiona's mood hardly improved. James put it down to post-natal depression, never guessing there might be deeper reasons for her dissatisfaction.

But it wasn't Eleanor she was tired of, the baby was not the source of her unhappiness, it was James. It was almost as if she was jealous of him, jealous that he could escape Eleanor's constant crying, jealous that he was still working, meeting people, making decisions when the only decision she had to make was what colour baby-grow she would wear today, and secretly jealous too of the fact that she had to share Eleanor with James at all. Irrational, yes – but that is how life is. Fiona decided that she needed to go back to work.

"But I thought you wanted to look after her yourself Fiona. I thought the Nanny was just to help us through the nights, I didn't realise you couldn't cope." James replied when she said she had to return to work or she would simply go mad.

"Cope? Is that what you think I am supposed to be doing?" Incredulous that he could be so unsympathetic. "Look at me for a moment. What do you see? I am forty-one years old and I have been trained to a very high degree, University, Chambers and several long years of hard slog. You might not realise it but my career was everything to me, at least it used to be. My life isn't suddenly over because I have given birth to a child. One day that child will go to school, what do you think I will be doing then?"

"Hey. Hey Fiona – where does all this anger come from? I am perfectly happy for you to go back to work, if that's what you want. It's just that we have never talked about it, that's all." He couldn't help it, every time he tried to help her he ended up apologising.

"We have never talked about anything James, that's the trouble." She seized on his weakness and turned the whole argument on him. "We drifted into everything, no plans at all. Sometimes I think the real reason you don't talk is because you don't have anything to say. No thoughts, no real opinions and very few emotions. You just don't talk about anything, do you?"

"Well that's hardly fair Fiona. I was simply happy to make you happy, that's why I never disagreed with anything. I thought that having this child and being a mother was what you wanted, but if going back to work will make you happy now, then fine, go back to work." Totally resigned now, he just wanted this nasty little spat to end.

"It's not about going back to work. We never, actually *you* never, want to talk about anything. You just smile but leave me to make all the difficult decisions. I sometimes feel that you aren't even here, even when I am talking to you I don't see anything in your eyes at all, not a flicker, not a spark of recognition that you are even there." Kick a man when he's down by all means, but don't be surprised if he kicks back now and then.

"I am always here Fiona. Here for you in every way." He said slowly but resolutely striving to make his point felt. "Hey, if you want me to argue with you – fine, I can argue, but we both know you don't really want that either do you. I can't help thinking you are just making all this up to justify your own actions, and I think that is quite beneath you, in fact you are being incredibly unfair. If I had "talked" as you say, we may have ended up rowing and hating each other, I felt it wiser to just be there for you. You once asked me to be there for you; that was all you wanted from me. Well, I am here for you now, simple as that."

"Fair or not, it's true." She harrumphed. "Maybe we shouldn't have got married, this has all been a bit too rushed, un-thought through. Oh, I don't know what I mean exactly. It's just not how I expected it to be." The tears were welling up in her eyes. "I'm not like all those other mums, pushing their sodding prams in the park with beaming smiles on their faces. I do love Eleanor. Of course I do, it's just not how I expected it to be."

"And somehow, that's my fault. Is that it?" He wanted to hold her, to take her in his arms, but he was still wary of this petulant Fiona he barely recognised.

"You always want to apportion blame, don't you? You should have been the lawyer, not me. I'm not saying it's your fault, I'm just not as happy as I thought I would be. And I don't really know why. So going back to work is my way of trying to get me, you know – Fiona, you must remember her, back."

Yes, he did remember her. And he missed her too; he just couldn't see a way back to how they used to be, before Eleanor, before the wedding, before bloody Buckinghamshire.

And so James put it all down to post-natal depression; he expected it to wear off in a few weeks or so. But Fiona knew it was something else. It was the start of the end, the rot was setting in, James was not the perfect man for her, she had been distracted by his good looks, his vagueness, his lack of any history, but she had been wrong; there was nothing behind that blank canvas, just more and even denser fog behind the fog. He definitely wasn't the right man for her – maybe there never would be one, God knows she had tried a fair few. But she had been wrong about James, she had mistaken his silence for some sort of deeper intelligence and understanding, but like most of the men she had known he simply had no conception of her, of what made her contented, of what motivated her, of how to make her happy. She couldn't quite convince herself that all she had wanted him for was as a father for her child, but somehow now that he had performed that task she had to admit that his limited usefulness was pretty much over. It was terribly sad, but he just wasn't the man she thought he might be.

And though he tried to fight it even James knew that it might indeed soon be over, there was something about her he couldn't understand; it was as if she was some sort of a stranger in the house. She looked like Fiona and talked like her, but the words she said were different. He kept looking for the Fiona he remembered, the one who loved sex, who kept her toothbrush hidden somewhere in his bathroom, who turned up at his flat with just a clean pair of knickers in her bag and an open smile. But he couldn't find her here in Buckinghamshire. In this really too large house with the live-in Nanny, he couldn't find the old Fiona at all. He was tired now all the time, tired of working, of smiling at potential clients he secretly despised, tired of endless strategy meetings that always ended up with the bleeding obvious – we need more clients - and he was tired of the hour and a half long journey twice a day, and now he was becoming tired of Fiona's constant complaining. If only he could rediscover her, return to that blissful existence they once had. But he had no answers to field against her constant questioning, he had no way of telling her how much he missed her even though a shadowy ghost of the woman he once thought he knew was right there in front of him, complaining about something he had done, or not done - he was never quite sure - besides he really was too tired to argue. Some mornings she would even start as he was dressing and it was a relief just to leave the house. He pulled the tie loose and unbuttoned his top shirt button as he breathed in the cold crisp morning air and strode off to the station. Leaving the car behind he enjoyed this half-hour walk, and besides it would delay his return in the evening. He dreaded returning to more arguments. At least this was real, this cold air, at least he felt alive as he shivered inside his new camel-hair coat.

Fiona negotiated a return to her old job and the nanny was given a large pay-rise and became permanent. But they would never again achieve that light touch their relationship had once had. They settled into a sort of make-believe marriage. They made believe that they were still in love, they made believe they were still happy, they made Fiona's family believe they were the perfect couple, they made their new-found suburban friends believe they had it all, the best of both worlds - but try as they might they couldn't make themselves believe any of it. And before Eleanor's fourth birthday they decided to break up, or rather Fiona did.

"It just isn't working James, is it?" she said late one night.

"Well it's not perfect I must admit. You never seem happy, or I cannot seem to make you happy, which may be the same thing - I really don't know any more. It doesn't matter what I try to do for you, none of it makes you happy. And that in turn makes me unhappy. I don't know what to do anymore. I don't know how to fix this thing, this wonderful thing we once had. And sometimes I feel that only one of us wants it to be mended anyway." He was resigned, he had nothing more to lose.

"Okay. It's all my fault. I should never have gotten pregnant. That's at the core of it, isn't it? If Eleanor hadn't come along we might all have been so happy. Is that it?"

"No, that isn't it. I cannot imagine my life without Eleanor in it now. I don't blame you for having her at all. I wouldn't un-have her for the world. I just never knew that we would end up like this. We barely talk to each other some days. You seem angry all the time, with me, with the child, with your job, with life itself it would seem. And I am both hopeless and helpless. My happiness depends on you being happy, and everything I do only seems to make you more unhappy. What is it you really want Fiona?"

"At the moment I don't want you, that's for sure. Sometimes I get so angry just looking at you I want to scream. I think that Eleanor and I would be happier on our own. I really think you should think about moving out. At least for a while, a couple of months maybe. I need a bit of space to get my head sorted out, to find out what I really want. Do you understand that?"

"To be honest I don't understand any of it. I certainly don't understand you Fiona. I am going to bed – I am tired and have a crucial meeting at eight tomorrow morning. I can't do this anymore." And happy just to escape to the oblivion of sleep, he sloped off and left Fiona sitting alone, the TV sound down and the heavy pencil-pleated curtains open as the heavy rain splattered down. All she could see was darkness and rain – and she longed for a little sunshine in her life.

And after a lot more conversations in the same vein they (or Fiona anyway) decided that James should move out (and James felt the easiest thing was to agree with her). Or Fiona left him with very little choice, or so he felt. He rented a one bedroom flat in Pimlico and he stayed there during the week. He came home at the weekends and they played happy families for a day or two. The excuse for family and friends was that James' company was in full-blown takeover talks with an American outfit, lots of late night meetings so he was staying up in town. At least James still saw Eleanor every weekend and that was some sort of consolation. But he knew everything was on the slide, and he knew only too well from childhood that at the bottom of the slide if you didn't slow yourself down you came to a very nasty bump.

They had stopped making love a few months ago, and anyway it had never been the same after the baby. They had to be quiet in case the Nanny heard, and somehow with someone else in the house it never seemed natural anymore. It became the opposite of what they once had, it almost became a duty – if they stopped making love what would they have left of a relationship at all. But of course they even stopped making love in the end. James didn't know how to suggest it, they slept in separate rooms, always had done, and if Fiona didn't instigate it, as she always had, then James didn't know how or was too scared to ask. Weeks turned into months and neither of them mentioned it. But it niggled at the back of James's mind. Another niggle added to his general unhappiness. Mostly he was so tired by it all, the sulks, the same old conversations and his own sense of helplessness that he just wanted sleep, but like most men he would wake at five in the morning burning with desire, and just as equally knowing that the object of his lust might just as well have been in another country as a few steps across the hall from his own bedroom.

Pimlico

So what did our Philanthropist think of all this, of this unexplained change in his beloved Fiona, his almost forced marriage and then being dispensed with once his usefulness as a father for her child was over? Actually he felt completely exhausted, drained of all emotion and rational thought. He couldn't quite understand what was happening to him. He felt like the victim of a car-crash, bruised and dazed, walking away from the wreckage but who couldn't remember the precise collision, or who was driving, or even where it hurt anymore. Sometimes he wasn't even sure that it did hurt, he had become immured to the pain; somehow his brain wasn't registering the suffering. He was actually quite depressed although he barely understood it at the time. He had entered a state of shell-shock where nothing really mattered anymore; he was still going through the motions, driving to the station, train up to town, meetings all day and then home to this half-life but almost on auto-pilot. His mind was numb, thoughts drifted in and out without really registering.

He tried seeking refuge in the old records of his youth, maybe he could find himself here in the music that had never let him down, but when he noticed that the album had finished he would slowly rouse himself, slide open the CD tray, lift the CD out and look at the disc with some surprise; he couldn't actually remember hearing any of it. He had stopped really listening to Fiona too, or whoever the woman was who looked and sounded like, but certainly wasn't, his darling Fiona, a while ago. It all seemed pointless, whatever he said was bound to be wrong so he spoke even less, simply walking away; which of course, and even he knew it but what could he do, simply made things worse. But how else could he recapture the Fiona he once had known and now missed so much; it was far too late for arguing, he had tried once to hold her, to wrap her in his arms but she shrugged him off with such obvious disdain that he never tried again. Patterns of behaviour had long since been established; Fiona decided and he went along with it; that was the way their relationship had always worked. Only now it wasn't working, and it was far too late and he was far too tired to change things.

Then he lost his job. His investment house was swallowed up by one of the big boys, mergers were happening everywhere as the City consolidated. The cover story he and Fiona had conjured up had suddenly materialised. He had been asleep at the meetings or hadn't really comprehended what was happening. It wasn't until it was over and all the papers signed that he discovered that there was to be no place for him in the new set-up. Somehow he had missed that in all the discussions. They gave him a cheque for three quarters of a million and a non-disclosure clause and everyone smiled and shook hands and our hero walked out of the door feeling as if he had been mortally wounded rather than given the biggest cheque he had ever held in his hands. He looked at it, not even sure how many noughts were attached; it could have been seventy-five thousand for all he cared. He folded it, slipped it in his pocket, shook the new owner's hands and walked all the way home. He walked along Cannon Street and down to the Embankment, gazing over the Thames at all the new buildings going up to the South. He somehow found himself back home and he still hadn't really understood how his life had disintegrated around him. He had no idea what to do next.

He turned his face to the wall. He returned to his one-bedroom flat in Pimlico, shrugged off his suit and shirt, tumbled into bed and pulled the covers up over his head and tried to sleep. He just wanted to clear his head of all thoughts, oblivion was what he needed. He was so fucking tired, if only sleep would come, and eventually after he had run everything over and over in his mind for what seemed the thousandth time sleep eventually overtook him. He slept for hours and hours and on waking he tugged the duvet higher and tried to fall back into that delightful oblivion again. And whenever he woke he simply wanted to sleep some more.

He had nothing to do, nothing to get out of bed for, nobody to talk to, nothing to think about even; he just tried to empty his tired brain of all thought. He turned his face to the wall and didn't get out of bed or wash or eat for over a week, drinking bottled water and pissing into a rancid saucepan by the side of the bed. He only got out of his stinking pit when he realised that the wretched saucepan would overflow if he pissed into it anymore. He stumbled to the bathroom and watched as a week's piss poured into the pan. Strangely he hadn't shit in all that time, but then he hadn't eaten either, or much at all for weeks before that either. He had lost weight but apart from tightening his belt a notch or two he had barely noticed. His face was gaunt and thin and he looked older but nobody had said anything to him and he hadn't really noticed. Though he had shaved every day he hadn't even noticed his haunted expression staring back at him.

Fiona had told him two days before he was paid off to leave them alone for a few weeks; she couldn't cope with his weekend visits anymore. It apparently was stressing them both out, though Eleanor simply seemed glad to see him, jumping into his arms with excitement as usual, though she did seem quite oblivious when he left, returning to her toys just that bit too enthusiastically. He had been in such a daze that he wasn't capable of thinking anything, this was just another blow, another stage in the deterioration of their relationship; he had been expecting something like this for weeks now. The weekend visits were just another part of the world someone else was planning for him; his only duty was to go along with it. And now even this tentative contact was being suspended; or stopped altogether – that was surely only a matter of time anyway. And he simply shrugged his shoulders and went along with it. Staring out of the car window he was surprised when the car pulled up outside his flat, he couldn't recall the journey at all. He couldn't remember who had been driving; but it must have been him, Fiona had never driven the Audi, she had always preferred her Merc. He had gone along with everything and everyone and now he felt so fucking miserable. No matter how many times he ran the memories of Fiona through his mind he couldn't quite see what he had done wrong, except fall for her in the first place. He knew that no matter how he had played the hand she had dealt him it would always end up being folded, his meagre chips scooped up as he was forced to leave the table. But despite his misery, despite his anger, his utter despair, he would have given anything to be back in their flat in Kensington, or on the beach with her at Barcelona, or just sitting opposite her at dinner watching as she folded away really quite substantial dinners into that pretty little mouth of hers.

He hauled himself out of his dirty bed and into the bathroom. He looked in the mirror and could hardly recognise himself. It wasn't just the beard, patchy and scratchy as it was, his eyes had huge bags under them and were red, his hair was greasy and lank and he looked old. God did he look old. He was only forty or so but he looked and felt at least fifty. Fifty? Approaching sixty even, who knew. He ran a basin of cold water and dipped his blotchy face in it. For a moment the thought crossed his mind that he should just leave his face submerged in that cool water. What a relief not to have to even breathe again; just let it be over now. But the survival instinct combined with a gagging reflex in the back of his throat forced his face out of the basin. He lifted his sad dripping face and looked again. One last chance, one last roll of the dice, let's just give it one more throw shall we? But different this time; no more bid for respectability, no stupid dalliances with women, and no mercy this time. None at all. He ran the hot water and tried to shave, the expensive five blade razor catching and pulling at the tough bristles. He had to shave three times to get anything like a smooth finish and still he cut himself a couple of times. He crawled into the shower and just let the hot water pound into his body, leaning against the white tiles he almost drifted back to sleep; then it was the loo, and surprisingly he pooh-ed. It was as if he was being cranked up again notch by notch and slowly his body started responding. Shaved, showered and shitted he felt a bit better. What the fuck had happened to him? That was his constant thought. All of this had happened with minimal input from himself; Fiona had called all the shots, but then she always had had her pretty little finger on the trigger, he just hadn't realised that he had been the target all along. He thought about calling her but his new-fangled mobile phone was almost dead, the charger left in an office he was no longer needed in. He tossed it aside. He hadn't spoken to her for eight days, and he saw he had no missed calls before the battery finally gave out, so she hadn't rung him either. And he knew then it was finally over. He had meant so little to her that she hadn't even called for eight fucking days. She might never phone him again – it wouldn't surprise him in the slightest. He was, for the first time in his whole relationship with Fiona beginning to get angry. And he knew that angry was good, it would help him recover. A little bit of hate helps the medicine go down; and God knows he had had to swallow enough of the stuff.

His crumpled Hugo Boss suit lay on the ground and he binned it along with the Gieves and Hawkes shirt and tie. He had plenty of others, but he pulled out an old pair of jeans and a tee-shirt. He sat in his armchair, yawned (surprisingly still tired after a week of sleep), thought about switching on the telly but reached for the CD controller. There was already a CD in the player. The Beatles White Album, an old favourite. As he sat back he sung quietly along to 'Back in the USSR'. And he felt a bit better. He still had the music and just as when he was a teenager The Beatles were singing just for him. "Get your balalaikas out - we're back in the USSR."

That phase of his life was over now. He had tried the respectable path and it hadn't worked. He had married her even, and that had made no difference at all. He thought all of that would make him happy but it had been diminishing returns, the more he gave the more it cost him the less he got in return. Happy? Had he ever been really happy? He thought back – had he been happiest selling records at Camden Market, or making up the compilation tapes he sold, or had he been happiest when he first came to London in that little bedsit with his first love lying warm by his side, or had it been in Wembley building that first successful car business? No, he had been happiest when he was a down and out, when he was sleeping rough on a sheet of cardboard behind Waterloo station. No friends, no lovers, no money, and no money worries either, and no identity at all. Free of all concerns. That was when he had been happiest. But there was no way he was returning to that existence. This time it was going to be different, this time he had a purpose.

He decided to call Richard, his old co-Director from the car and property days. He needed a favour. He still had his number somewhere.

"Richard, it's James here – you remember, James Pilkington."

"Of course – and how could I forget you old boy? I hear you have been doing rather well, quite the City whizz-kid, sold out for nigh on a mill or something like that."

"Not quite, but actually Richard I need a small favour, can we meet."

The Philanthropist

And over coffee in Soho, Richard slipped him a small page ripped from his filofax with a number and the name "Bill" on it.

"Don't mention my name when you speak to him, just say a mutual friend. After that you are on your own." Richard said quietly as he handed the slip of paper over.

"Richard – I've never told anyone but I have always been on my own, and never more so than now." James admitted. "I never really thanked you for Wembley, or rather for the opportunity. I think I was at least as responsible as you for our success, but thanks anyway." And added as an afterthought "And I promise I won't bother you ever again."

"Well that's a strange way of saying thank you, but you always were a strange one James. I hear that you are married now, may I at least congratulate you?"

"Congratulations can be put on hold for a while as I will almost certainly be getting divorced soon." His coffee spoon clanking in the saucer seemed to deaden the very air around them.

"Oh, I am sorry to hear that." Richard said, though he hadn't thought of James in years. But what else can you say?

"So life goes, Richard. So it goes"

And they left the small coffee-shop in Soho separately and never saw each other again. Richard never realised he had been talking to the Philanthropist and even when the news of his amazing Philanthropy was all over the news he never guessed either. In fact none of his former acquaintances ever guessed; not his first love, wherever she was now - or Joan, the woman with an unspoken past who had rescued him from the streets, or any of the escort girls (just another faceless punter) or even Fiona. Just as Fiona had accused James of not understanding anything about her, so she had never understood anything about James either. And that's far more common than you think.

She actually did indeed divorce him soon after this and she got almost everything, Eleanor of course, the house in Buckinghamshire and a decent alimony. Except the pay-off money that is; that non-disclosure clause came in quite handy. He didn't contest anything, happy to agree the generous monthly payments and he had never liked the big house in Buckinghamshire anyway, and he never saw Fiona or his daughter again.

It was a huge wrench, but he knew he had to do it. He had a plan and he could only accomplish that plan without any baggage at all, especially emotional. Much as he loved Eleanor, and Fiona too in a way, it was easier this way. Better to cut out the cancer than keep going back for heart-rending treatment time and time again. Just like that time after returning from Edinburgh when he bundled his first love, pregnant and dazed, into the taxi and let her go to face the world on her own. This time it was almost easier, Fiona was the instigator, he simply had to disappear. Besides he knew he might not be strong enough if he saw that little girl's face again, and he needed to be strong, stronger than he had ever been in his life if he wanted to carry out his plans. He had to disappear again so he arranged for all his correspondence to be handled by a small secretarial agency who kept enquirers away because they literally knew nothing. He phoned them once a week and called in to collect any mail. They had no idea where he lived and to the rest of the world he simply became invisible. His lawyer's letters and e-mails were answered promptly; they only had the agency address but he paid them promptly so no questions were asked. He actually moved to South London, to Morden – not really London at all. It was at the very Southern end of the Northern line and he felt that this was suitably obscure, and almost a joke. Many was the time he had watched as trains pulled into tube stations with Morden as their destination, never imagining it would become his one day. Morden was the end of the line. But actually the Philanthropist was only just getting started.

Morden

Paul Wilson settled into his new one-bedroom flat in Morden, he had bought it for fifty thousand, a cash buyer. The last owner had left his furniture behind and this secretly pleased Paul; another person's taste was even better, and besides no-one would be invited back here, no girlfriends and no escorts either – he had tired of that game long ago. He bought a fairly cheap hi-fi (he had once had the very best Bang and Olufssen systems, but now he actually preferred hearing music on cheap systems, that's how he remembered it as a teenager, when the speakers couldn't quite handle the bass and rumbled, that's what he liked to hear) and arranged for his music, mostly Vinyl but quite a few CDs and cassettes too, which had never been taken out of storage after they sold the Kensington apartment, to be delivered. He had always been a North London boy; he had never considered South London at all. It might as well be a foreign country, but nothing like that bothered him at all now.

The first thing he did with his new identity was to set-up a limited company; in fact he set up rather a lot of limited companies. And the directors he chose to run these companies were all new identities too. "Bill" had come in rather handy and at a grand a pop he was cheap enough too. He rented a very plush office in the West End, just North of Oxford Circus and hired a secretary and an accounts clerk and had computers installed and all the trappings of a small but successful business. He had spent nearly half of his pay-off money, but that was okay. Money was to now take on a different meaning entirely; money now had a purpose, money was no longer for personal gratification, although maybe a very small amount might be used for that. Money was now to be used to attract money.

He never showed himself at the office, he communicated by phone or this new-fangled e-mail. Nobody ever saw Paul Wilson or any of the other Directors.

"Yes, Mr. Wilson, I understand, and I will e-mail that over to you straightaway"

E-mail was the new thing. It was amazing, you could be anywhere, or almost anywhere, in the world and as long as you had an internet connection you could send and receive messages and documents. It could have been designed precisely for such a one as him, where anonymity and facelessness were the most desirable of assets. He could, in theory, never leave his flat, though of course he would have to, to be successful that is.

He met his clients in hotels all over the world; he would rent the rooms by the day. He schmoozed them over lunch and then they retired to discuss business in his private suite. And the business they discussed was Money; or rather how to make money grow and more importantly how to hide money (from business associates, from ex-wives and most of all from the taxman). He chose his clients carefully and took time to check them out, or sometimes he used private detectives to find out just how they had become wealthy in the first place, which schools they had been to, what divorce settlements they had negotiated and most importantly how greedy they were.

"So exactly how does it work? I mean. You say that I will get twenty per cent every year; come what may. Sounds a bit implausible to me."

"Actually most years we will of course make far more than the twenty percent I will pay to you. Rather than take a commission I prefer to have to work harder to make sure that I make much more for me than I give to you." Paul smiled as he added the killer-blow. "You don't think I am in this game for nothing do you? I love money as much as anyone."

"So why don't you just use your own money, if you can get such a good return on it, I mean."

"Because I don't have enough of my own yet. When I do I will stop using other people's money. I reckon it will take me ten years or so to get where I want to be, then I can give you and the few other investors back their money and walk away with a cool ten billion myself."

"But this must be illegal, surely. Why don't I have my Accountants take a look at your organisation before I decide?"

"I can assure you that we are perfectly legal and our books are audited and we pay our taxes, it is just that the way we operate both you and our few lucky investors end up paying almost no tax on the real profits. You must realise also that your Accountants will keep coming up against brick walls (we hide our tracks very well) and they will advise you not to invest," Again that complicit smile from Paul, "Which of course is the very reason that you will. If they were half as clever as us you wouldn't be talking to me now. We are a totally independent privately owned entity; it will take the best Auditors years to find out even the barest details, that is of course why we are so successful." Then the pause, the buttoning of his suit and the gathering up of the papers, "Actually if you are still having doubts maybe it is best that I just walk away and pretend we never had this discussion. It has been nice talking to you but I cannot waste any more time, I have lots of other people to see."

"Don't be so hasty. What is the minimum investment I can make?"

"At the moment that stands at one hundred mill. Pounds sterling that is, not dollars. It goes up every year as the organisation grows. Of course there is the usual caveat that as this is an investment freely entered into by both parties there is no guarantee of any returns and your investment may be lost. But that's just for the lawyers. The twenty percent is my personal promise to you."

"One hundred million? That's a lot of money."

"Listen. You are very successful, and part of that success is down to your utter ruthlessness. We both know what I am talking about. And I am sure you will know just how to find me if I should ever let you down, so rest assured I won't. Why don't you just try it for a year to begin with; I will forward transact one hundred and twenty back to you, payable one year from now, and then we can talk again about you investing a serious amount. Or we can start out as we mean to carry on, trusting one another and both making some serious money."

"What makes you think that a hundred million is not a serious amount for me?"

"Because my friend I happen to know that you are worth almost four billion on paper; and probably far more than that in reality. I won't play games with you, so don't play games with me. You have consistently hidden most of your wealth in off-shore accounts paying almost no tax but receiving at best ten percent. As you know I will guarantee you twenty, think about it – double what you are getting now. If you want to invest let me know. I have to be leaving soon; I am flying to St. Petersburg tomorrow. The offer will remain on the table for seven days. You know how to contact me. Let's speak again before then."

And so they usually invested. A few backed off, but secretly regretted it. He had started off asking for five million minimum, but had soon raised this, and the more he asked for the easier it seemed to be. Greed by its very nature is incremental too; what gambler doesn't dream of huge winnings if only they had a big enough stake. Secrecy was written into the contracts, absolute non-disclosure. But the Philanthropist knew that this was another secret weapon and that despite having promised not to, most would inevitably tell their best friends (in the strictest confidence), who would of course contact him sooner or later. After a while he was fending potential investors off rather than having to woo them. It was like a secret party that everyone wanted to be invited to. And the harder it was to get in the more they wanted it.

New York and Morden

Because he never gave up his little flat in Morden, and every so often Paul Wilson would return from his plush New York base and come home, hanging up his expensive Pierre Cardin suits and tucking away his handmade shoes and would drag on a pair of old jeans and a T-shirt and slip on a record and settle back to listen to The Stones or The Who or one of the old bands from his youth. These were the times he was most happy and it was here among the records (now mostly on CD) of his youth that he kept all the records of his various companies too. They were all there in foolscap blue ledgers, each book representing a client and the amount he (they were almost all he's) had "invested," where the funds had been distributed and what returns had been earned, and what sums paid back to the investor. And which company had "leant" which company how much, and exactly where that money had gone. It was all done in initials, but not quite, as our Philanthropist had his own nicknames for most of his greedy clients. If some future historian should ever come across these neat blue ledgers they would have some difficulty in de-ciphering his tiny spidery writing, much as those reading the original Pepys diaries a couple of centuries ago must have felt.

He never actually accepted that there was any element of theft involved. As far as he was concerned he never stole any money. Misappropriation might be a better word for it, and when his plans came to their full fruition no-one could really accuse him of stealing, and certainly not for his own benefit. Redistribution certainly, a moral paying back of past debts maybe; and after all he had always warned them that any investment may be risky. Besides he justified himself in that most of the fortunes he was playing with had never been taxed properly and had quite possibly been ill-gotten at the very least. Inherited money was almost always stolen or the proceeds of slavery or theft of land in the past, respectability was the hardest thing to buy yet it was almost the most sought after. And who was he anyway; his aliases were the ones moving money about surely. It was almost as if he didn't exist at all, it was all done in the name of others, even though it was all recorded precisely in his ledgers (well someone had to keep the records). He felt no guilt; he was only doing to his investors what they or their families had done to others. He was quietly re-arranging the world. No different really from hiding the tooth paste or substituting Reveille for Woman's Weekly on his paper round, it was all a game – he was just stepping up to another level.

Of course his multiple companies and accountants were doing the same thing, keeping records, in their own various companies, it was just that like the spider at the centre of his web he was the only one who knew exactly how it all fitted together. Most of the companies had no idea they were linked in any way; different Directors, different locations, different banks. Only Paul or whoever he chose to call himself on any particular day knew how the jigsaw fitted together, and even he had to regularly refer back time and again to those neat blue ledgers.

His clients were happy, that was all that mattered. They had their dividends paid discreetly into hidden bank Accounts, some in Switzerland and many in the middle East or tiny island states that were once part of the British Empire but which now made so much money by being respectable and yet disreputable at one and the same time. A few clients believing quite sensibly that this couldn't possibly continue forever asked for their "investment" back. No problem at all, the money was transferred straight away. He never tried to dissuade anyone; after all it was their money. Confidence was everything and the more happy customers who would tell their rich friends that the money was safe, that you could get it out whenever you wanted, just a phone call and it was done, the better. Though why, when you were getting twenty percent guaranteed and tax-free would you possibly want to take your money out. In five years you got it all back anyway and the capital was 'safe' and still earning you money.

And so the empire grew. After a few years there was so much money coming in that Paul was spending most of his time just investing it. Diversification was the key, some was in dubious Russian start-ups, newly "Privatised" industries that had languished under Communism but were now booming. Paul invested in the Far East too; China was a sleeping giant that was just beginning to embrace Capitalism, if you knew the right people there were fortunes to be made. Some money was invested in America, in new tech start-ups; college kids eager to accept half a million dollars for 51% as long as they were left alone to develop ideas on their computers, many failed but some made it big. Who would have thought a stupid name like Facebook or Google would ever catch on. Maybe he was lucky, or just that tiny bit more reckless than if it has been only his own money; after all if it all came crashing down he would walk away and Paul Wilson would be searched for but never found. And so Paul's conglomeration, or actually more a Gulag of companies, thrived.

Of course even with this diversification there was no way that twenty percent was really achievable, or not reliably so. Some years he came close but there were bad years too, but like all Ponzi schemes it was the ever-growing piles of new money coming in at the bottom that kept the dividends flowing for those at the top. Yes, a Ponzi scheme it was, though it did appear, on paper at least, to be making profits (well if you conveniently forgot about the investors initial deposits of course). Though of course that is exactly how all banks and investment companies work; if everyone asked for their money back at the same time the whole thing would tumble down like a house of cards. This was what almost happened in 2008 when Lehman Brothers collapsed, but Governments all over the world stepped in and propped up the most fragile and overloaded dominoes just in time to stop the cascade in its' tracks. Though some would argue that the ripples were still being felt and as usual it would be the poor who paid for the follies of the rich. Ah, glorious Capitalism – what a system and what a disgrace. So it goes.

But the Philanthropist had managed to spread his companies so cleverly that even if there were a run on any one particular "investment" company there would be nothing linking it to the others, or at least it might take years to untangle the web. And on one level the Philanthropist was perfectly legal, he happily paid taxes in whichever country his companies were set up in. It was just that no-one ever realised that the inter-company loan accounts were never repaid, or no-one ever queried the huge sums involved. Governments were so happy to receive Corporation tax that nobody was asking the right questions. Besides, no money had been borrowed from banks, it was all private investors and each company was relatively small, so no-one put it all together and worked out what was happening.

Paul knew of course that it must collapse at some point. In fact it had come close in the few days after Lehman imploded, when quite a few "investors" wanted out. Paul was constantly flying from St.

Petersburg to Beijing to New York to transfer large sums around, but he got through that scare. After the initial few large withdrawals things settled down, and as banks were now forced to be far more careful he was flooded with greedy new investors wanting a piece of the security and high dividends he was promising. The very fact that he had survived where many had fallen made him that much more desirable. The very essence of the market, that that which everyone wanted demanded the highest price, meant that he was now sought out rather than having to woo clients as he had had to at first. Greed, oh wonderful greed, was now the driver, and all Paul had to do was hang on to the steering wheel a bit longer. Of course he had to be even more careful who he chose now, rejecting far more than he accepted, which only served to increase demand.

By 2020 he had huge sums, undreamt of sums, piling up; easily enough to pay the annual dividends and billions more than that too. The banks were in terminal decline, many in Europe were being propped up by National Governments or the EU itself. Ever more rigorous controls were being placed on them, all in the name of protecting the public. Where else was any self-respecting entrepreneur supposed to put his money? It would soon be time to act.

He set up even more companies, this time property companies. He had missed out on the property booms of the nineties and the 2010's, but he had also avoided the crashes. Time to get into property, but this time however he was buying property for an entirely different purpose, he didn't care what happened to house prices.

But what, you may ask, ever happened to Fiona and Eleanor? How did Paul manage to forget them, to cut them out of his life so completely? It was actually made easier by Fiona's innate selfishness; she was quite happy at first to simply lose contact with James. It suited her that all the dealings were between lawyers; she understood the legal world. It was finite and clear, no ambiguities, no changing of minds, no emotional hang-ups, no lying and subterfuge (except that inherent in the industry and which she was completely comfortable with). Besides, the money kept coming in; James managed to pay her handsomely and whenever her lawyers hit him for more funds, when Eleanor needed to go to a very expensive Private school or to University he happily paid the bills – after all, it wasn't exactly his money anyway.

Fiona resumed her old job and her old habits with remarkable ease. She joined a few dating sites, and enjoyed the convenience and the anonymity of these encounters; the excitement of being "chatted up," when it was inevitable that she was going to fuck the guy anyway. And afterwards how easy it was to just drop him an e-mail "Let's take a rain-check, shall we? I'll let you know when I want to see you again." She played some along for a time, while it was still fun, but the one thing she was certain of was that never again would she have a relationship. James had cured her of that. She had invested far too much time and energy on that one, and he had turned out to be just like all the others in the end, a sad little loser.

Still, she had her lovely daughter so all in all it may have been worth it. But in a strange way as the child grew into a little girl and then a feisty teenager Fiona felt less and less of an emotional tie to her; the boarding school was a God-send; at least she only had to deal with this independently minded individual in the holidays. And her own mother and father were only too willing to spend their twilight years entertaining their only grandchild. The very thing she had once wanted, needed above everything else, her own child, had grown up and as each year passed they slowly grew apart. That little baby which she had so prettily dressed each day no longer needed her mother. Fiona, when she stopped a moment to question her own motives, felt that it had been necessary. She had had to have a child; else she would have always been left with that question mark, what if? But as so often in life when she finally got what she desired it turned out that it wasn't quite what she had thought it would be. So it goes.

Eleanor of course was the one most affected by the break-up. No matter how bad the parents may feel they almost always get over it; it's the children who suffer. She could never quite understand how one day her father had been there, loving her, worshipping her in fact -and then he was gone. Nobody bothered to explain to the five-year old that her father simply didn't want to know her anymore. And even when they did she couldn't accept that he had simply decided to stop loving her, something must have happened to make him leave her. She carried around the memory of him and his betrayal of her for years. Sometimes she blamed him and sometimes she blamed her mother, but mostly she decided it must have been her fault, something she had done, something she had maybe been unaware of, but she, Eleanor, must have been the instigator, she must have been the one who caused him to stop loving her. She would make up little plays with her expensive dollies, rehearsing them through the trauma of losing one or even both parents. She avidly watched soaps like Eastenders and Hollyoaks and related to all the young women when they were treated harshly by their men. But all this time she was moving further away from her mother too (Fiona leaving her more and more with her grandparents); how unlucky she thought to have been abandoned by both parents, neither really wanting to spend time with her. In some way this became a support for her, a reassurance of her own inadequacy perhaps; there is a strange comfort to be had in the knowledge that you are utterly alone, that nobody loves you.

By the time she went to University she was sure she wanted to be a lesbian and tried to get into it; she loved the attention she got from other girls, the gay clubs and the excitement of meeting real lesbians - it was just that the inevitable sex left her cold. Emotionally she couldn't bear the idea that she might actually be straight, men were rubbish, her own father had walked out on her, she loved girls and she wanted to be loved by girls, men were definitely not her thing – but she didn't really enjoy all that licking and kissing - it all left her strangely empty. It was all okay when it was shopping and dinners and drinking and with each new partner she hoped against hope that the sex would move her this time. Eventually she allowed herself to trust a boy and though she was right, he was indeed an idiot as she had suspected, she did quite enjoy the sex. Her brain fought the pleasure she was experiencing, surely this was wrong; she almost felt guilty for enjoying it. Confused, it would take her a few more years to realise that she actually wanted sex with men but not the relationship with the man himself, (much like her dear mother). Maybe she was still looking for her father, or the emotional link she had lost while rejecting him at the same time. People have always been confused about sex and relationships, frantic selfish little monkeys that we are, never happier than when we are unhappy. She did try when she was in her early twenties to find her father, but her attempts came to nothing. It was as if he had disappeared from the face of the earth completely. One time she tried to talk to her mother about him.

"It's as if he never existed" she said, "or has just up and moved to another country."

"But he was always elusive, your father. That was one of the reasons we broke up." Fiona agreed, "You see, I never actually found out who he was. I sometimes think I may even have invented him."

"What do you mean, invented him? He was real enough surely." queried Eleanor.

"Real? Yes he was real I suppose; physically he did exist, but I never got into his head, I never found out what made him tick. And he had no history at all. He once said to me, about his past 'It is as if I was a totally different person then, I wouldn't recognise me myself now.' And that is just how he was I am afraid, no past, and a strangely elusive present – I never felt I really ever knew him, and now he has disappeared again, become someone else entirely I expect." she said, not realising the truth of her glib remark. "Oh I tried to find out about him but it was as if he was simply a name on paper, there was never anyone who even pretended to know him. In some ways that was the allure; I was always trying to discover exactly who he was, but sooner or later one tires of even that. And then when it ended he simply vanished. We split up and I never saw him again. In many ways it was easier that way, but I can never forgive him for abandoning you. Whatever he felt or in fact did not, maybe could not, feel for me, I always thought that he had loved you."

"I know what you mean, and I seem to remember that I loved him too, though I may have imagined that, who knows? Who can really remember how you felt at five? I've done internet searches and he doesn't seem to be anywhere, no known employment, he doesn't own any property and is on no electoral registers either. I used to think he must be dead, but surely there would be some record of that even."

"Yes, I've done that too. Only the money kept coming in until you grew up, so he must have been doing something. His solicitors knew as little as we did, or weren't telling, which ends up the same thing. He apparently had almost no contact with them either, but the money came in each month to pay both them and us so they didn't really care." She sighed. "And to tell the truth, neither do I?"

"I know that I shouldn't, after the way he wanted nothing to do with me, but actually I do care. I really would like to find him, if only to slap his face. Hard. Just the one time. I would dearly love to give him a damn good slap." Eleanor said with some venom in her voice.

"Ha, I used to feel like that, but not anymore. After all he gave me you. So he couldn't have been all bad, could he?" Fiona said, but no she had never wanted to slap him, in some ways he was the best thing that had ever happened to her, if only he hadn't taken up so much of her precious time.

Disingenous as ever; though clever at passing off an air of lazy contentment, Fiona too was quite unhappy. Somehow her career, which used to be everything to her, was boring her more and more as each year passed. She was successful, or as successful as she might ever have expected to be, it was just that it all seemed more than a bit pointless. She was making really good money, but there were only so many expensive holidays, so many investment flats to buy, so many ridiculously expensive couture clothes to buy, so many new men to fuck. She sometimes wondered what it was all for, but like most of us – she was on a treadmill, and for her the spending of the money had become as much of a treadmill as the earning it. She just couldn't quite find the courage to stop pedalling. So it goes.

But what of our hero, our dear Philanthropist? How was he coping, how did he manage without either Fiona or Eleanor? The truth is that just like his former identities he simply put them behind him. Like a snake shedding its skin each new body slithered free from the constrictions of the past and never looked back. Not exactly a mistake, more a diversion from his true path. They were in the past, in some way they no longer belonged to him. He managed to convince himself that everyone was selfish, we all used people but few had the courage he had to move on. Besides he was incredibly busy. Meetings with new clients, meetings with the Accountants or Bankers of his various companies, just keeping track of which company owed which exactly how much money, transferring vast sums or sending the e-mails to Accountants to transfer the money – all of this took up hours every day. And he never had a day off either, after all it would only leave him time for reflection. And that was the last thing he wanted to do. He had quite quickly resumed using escort girls again, (old habits, even though he had resolved not to, have a habit of dying not hard but very slowly) but this too had at last palled. The excitement was less and less, the girls were the same the world over, too pretty, too false and ultimately too boring. The services were the same; there was really very little variation. He really needed something else, something he had almost managed to find with Fiona. But he would never make that mistake again. He would never fall in love again, he would never trust anyone again the way he had trusted Fiona.

One day in New York a couple of evening meetings were cancelled. There were heavy snowfalls and JFK was closed. He had hours to kill and in his least favourite city. Despite being mostly based here he had that innate English distaste for and disdain of American self-confidence, the brashness of their architecture, the speed of their decision making, their lack of Anglo-Saxon diffidence at times appalled him. In a way it half-justified his taking their money, as if they deserved to be taught a lesson, if only to remind them that they were not God's chosen people. Bored by the multi-channels in his hotel room he decided to go for a walk. He wandered over to Broadway and nearly went into a show, but he knew he wouldn't enjoy it. The few musicals he had seen appalled him; so contrived, so ridiculously enthusiastic; and Opera too he hated, all that strutting around the stage in elaborate costumes, and usually sung in bloody Italian too.

He noticed the hookers in their miniskirts, shiny handbags and five-inch heels, tottering from car to car plying their trade. No, he didn't want that either. He had tried the dangerous side of prostitution, fucking in alleyways or in the back of a limo while his driver slowly drove round and round the block, and while the danger of being caught held a certain attraction this too was a short-lived pleasure. In fact sex itself was beginning to bore him, he was over seventy now and wondered if that was it – the dimming of the light, the fading of desire until even that buzz, that tingle, would disappear too. But no, he still felt he wanted something, he just wasn't sure what. He wanted something different, something he had never quite managed to experience and heaven knows he had experienced a lot. He saw a phone booth with little cards printed up advertising various call-girls or models as they liked to be called. Looking around him, he snatched a few and tucked them into his coat pocket. Back at his expensive hotel he pulled them out and discarded most. One however caught his eye. It was for BDSM. He was knowledgeable enough to realise this must mean bondage, domination and sado-masochism. He tapped the card on the glass coffee table a few times and began to ask himself if that might interest him. He had never liked pain, it was a nuisance, a sign that something wasn't right, a trigger to call a doctor. No, he had never enjoyed pain at all. Still the idea of being dominated was interesting. He booted up his laptop and soon found a few websites showing short clips of guys being tortured, having hot wax dripped on their dicks, or being clamped by the nipples. No, that wasn't what he wanted. Besides they looked ridiculous in those gimp masks and all that leather and spiked collars – all too staged for him. But still the idea of being dominated intrigued him. Hesitantly he rang the number.

"Hello" an educated, almost posh voice answered.

"I saw your card" he hesitatingly spoke "in a phone booth."

"And?" she sounded bored, as if she were being interrupted, not the one doing him a service "Just what is it you expect from me."

"I was wondering just what your services might be?"

"My services?" she said "I think you misunderstand me my dear. If you wish me to spend some time with you I can assure you that you will be the one servicing me, and the one paying for my pleasure too, not the other way round."

"I see. And exactly how much would that cost me?"

"That depends. Where are you calling from? I only see men in *expensive* Hotels."

"How does the Intercontinental Plaza sound, is that expensive enough for you?"

"It will do. My fee is one thousand dollars which you will transfer to my bank account. I will not step one foot out of my apartment until I see the amount transferred. Is that understood?"

"And what guarantee do I have that you will turn up at all? You could simply be running a scam for all I know."

"Don't be such a child. Transfer the money and I'll be there in an hour. And don't phone me again, I can't bear time-wasters. I will text you the account details and then an acknowledgement that funds have been received and you may then text me back your preferred time for your appointment. Understood?"

"Yes, I look forward to your text." Appointment, he thought – that's an interesting way to describe it.

"You should be looking forward to far more than that." And with that she hung up.

He laughed and tossed the phone on the sofa beside him. This was one woman he would not be rushing to meet. A thousand dollars? Was she crazy? But something still intrigued him, was it her chutzpah, her brazenness or her apparent contempt for him? She was certainly dominant, but was she what he wanted? Was she what he needed? Before he had time to really consider his phone beeped and he saw the incoming text.

She arrived quite promptly and texted him that she was in the lobby and was hungry, could he take her in to dinner. So, not a complete scam, though he wouldn't have been surprised if after taking his (or somebody's) money she had never contacted him again. But maybe it takes a scammer to appreciate a good scam. He dressed quickly and took the lift into the lobby.

She was stunning he had to admit that. Stunning - without looking like a slut (though in a different time and place he quite like the slutty look, the carelessly applied make-up, the bra straps showing, the too-short skirt, the frazzled hair and the smell of cheap cologne). This woman wore just the right amount of make-up so that it appeared she wore no make-up at all. An expensive suit, off white linen and beautifully cut, emphasising, but not too much, her very desirable body. Her dark short hair was expensively feather-cut and she wore a simple gold necklace, watch and bracelet, no rings and no ear-rings. To all appearances she was a businesswoman, maybe in Media or Advertising. No-one would ever have taken her for a call-girl.

She hardly acknowledged him but stood up as he approached and shook his hand in a strangely business-like way, and led the way to the Dining Room. She talked to the Head Waiter and requested a quiet table where they would not be disturbed, he followed dumbly behind her. After ordering for both of them, fillet steak, salad and a glass of expensive Claret she leaned in close to him and said.

"Understand this. From this moment on you are my slave. I will tell you exactly what to do. Your pleasure is no concern of mine but you will obey me in everything. Everything. I will direct you and I will be satisfied. Is that understood?"

"Yes, though I must say …" he began.

She cut him short. "I am not interested in anything you have to say. You will not speak unless I request it. If you speak again without my permission I will simply get up and leave. You have been warned. Okay?"

"Yes, I suppose so."

"Good. Now eat up that steak, you are going to need the stamina."

He paid the bill and she walked to the lift, turning only to say. "Two steps behind me. And do not attempt to touch me unless I instruct you to."

Once in the bedroom she told him to undress and shower. "If you wish to pleasure me I insist on cleanliness." He came back with a towel wrapped around him.

"Now undress me, slowly. One button at a time, don't fumble or rush things. Concentrate on the job in hand, and do not stroke me or try to touch my tits or cunt."

He did as he was told. She was exquisitely beautiful. She had small breasts with nipples that jutted out and a rounded pouty little arse with just a whisper of pubic hair trailing above a crinkly vagina that peeped out of soft folds of skin. He immediately had an erection, he desperately wanted to touch her or for her to touch him but he knew he would have to wait. She had warned him and the tone of her voice left him in no doubt that if he transgressed in the slightest she would leave. The anticipation, the waiting for permission was excruciating but incredibly exciting too, he was almost trembling. Normally with a call-girl she would be on her knees by now with his cock stuffed in her mouth, trying to make him come as quickly as possible. This woman had not touched him at all, she had made him slowly undress her but had studiously ignored his stonking erection. He had no idea what would happen next and that was what was so thrilling.

"Take that towel off and lay on the bed. Keep your hands by your sides, palms flat on the sheet and do not attempt to touch me in any way. If you lift your hands from your sides I will stop, get dressed and our time together will be over. Understood?" and she looked straight into his eyes, all he could do was silently nod his agreement.

She started to stroke his body, light strokes barely touching him, then she lent over his chest whispering over his nipples, her nipples grazed his stomach and down to his groin and back up again to his own. His erection became even harder as her hands slid to within inches of his dick. Tantalising close without actually touching him, she licked and sucked his nipples and brushed her own against his straining cock. Then she straddled his face and he was instructed to lick her out, just using his mouth. One of his hands involuntarily lifted to touch her on the hips. She slapped him hard across the face. Whack. She briskly stood up, walked to the door and leaning against it, spoke to him.

"I told you not to touch me. I am in control. I am the one who will be pleasured. Your task is to satisfy me. You will obey me or I shall leave. That is your last warning. Do not speak, just nod that you agree." She commanded.

He was shocked, that slap had really hurt, no-one had hit him since schooldays. She had really slapped him hard, his cheek tingled but he knew now he had no choice. He nodded. She resumed her position, and after what seemed an age, his tongue was aching, she seemed to have some sort of spasm. She lifted herself from his still stinging face and moved backwards and mounted him, slowly sliding herself onto his straining cock. She just sat there impaling herself on him. She warned him again.

"Do not thrust up to meet my movements. Simply lie there, I will do the fucking. Your job is to stay hard until I am finished. Understand? Nod."

He nodded and somehow resisted the temptation to push his hips up to meet hers. She came after a few minutes but carried on riding him. She reached out and put one finger to his lips.

"You are not to come. Is that understood? Be under no illusion, I will not wank you or suck you off or allow you to come in my presence. If you come I will leave and never return no matter how much money you offer me. I am not that sort of woman. You may wank when I have gone. Nod."

This was quite simply the most incredible sexual experience he had ever had. The sensations just kept flowing but did not rise to a climax. In fact he felt no urge to come at all; he was simply enjoying the experience too much. This was so different, it was another level completely. He never wanted it to stop.

"I will stop in ten minutes" she said looking at her gold watch, her tits bouncing with each thrust. "Nod."

He nodded.

"I will grant you one favour. Would you like that? Nod."

He nodded.

"Would you like me to piss in your mouth? Nod."

The thought had never entered his head before. He had always hated the smell of pee, his own included, and yet suddenly that was what he wanted more than anything else. Whatever she wanted he knew he would have to agree to. He needed her to command him, he needed to obey her. He nodded, the nod had been involuntary; he had surrendered any resistance with that first slap. Whatever she had suggested he would have nodded.

"Are you ready? Nod."

And then she raised herself off his cock with a noisy thwocking sound and leaning backwards she brought her wet cunt up towards his face and let go a tiny stream of pee. As the hot liquid splattered onto his face she said "Drink it,"

He obediently opened his mouth and swallowed her hot pee. It was like drinking hot bitter and salty black tea, but he barely noticed the taste. She stopped almost as soon as she had started. "That will do for your first training. This is your first time, isn't it? Nod."

And he nodded.

"But it won't be your last, will it? You really love being my slave don't you? You enjoy being used, you love it when I tell you what to do, don't you? Nod?

He nodded. Of course he loved it; it was simply the most amazing feeling, relinquishing all control to her. Subsuming his own desires, being dictated to; he would nod for a thousand years if she demanded it. She got off the bed and he tried to sit up. One hand pushed him firmly back, "I didn't say you could move. Stay where you are until I say you may get up. And don't touch that ridiculous cock of yours until I have gone either."

She dressed slowly, watching him all the time and turned to him one hand on the door handle.

"You may wank when I have gone. Nod."

He nodded.

"If you would like to continue your training you know my number. Nod."

And she was gone. She had been in his room for over an hour but he hadn't touched her exquisite body once. He had been forbidden to at first, but then strangely the desire had passed. This was so incredible he lay on the bed stunned for several minutes, his erection had subsided. He didn't even want to wank now; the experience had been enough in itself. It was the being totally in her control that had been so exciting. He had no idea that she would pee on him, that had been a complete surprise; and even now the idea repulsed him, but at the time he had gone along with it, the fact that she had dictated it had made it desirable. He had no idea that she wouldn't let him come; all the call-girls he had used had tried to get him to come as quickly as possible; he had had to struggle to hold himself back to get his money's worth. This was so different. It wasn't even the sex really. Yes, the sensations with her riding him but not allowing him to thrust up had been marvellous, but it had been sensation without an end. Always before any sexual activity had sooner or later led to his ejaculation and then it was over, and he simply wanted them to leave. As quickly as possible, he couldn't wait to shove them out of the door. Fiona had sometimes cuddled up to him but had soon retired to her own bed, and he never wanted the escort girls to stay, even though a few offered him seconds. He couldn't wait to get rid of them. As soon as he had come he felt a sort of disgust, both for them and for himself and just wanted to be on his own again. With this woman - and he hadn't even had the chance to ask her name, he never wanted it to end. In fact the very fact of her not offering so much as a name made it that much more exciting; the anonymity of the whole thing – just a phone number was the only tentative connection. He was tempted to call her, to speak to her, to hear her imperious tone of voice again, but he was scared she would simply put the phone down on him or tell him that that he had blown it, that that one time had been his only time with her and that no amount of money transferred would make her change her mind. He knew he would call her again the next time he was holed up in this wretched city; he simply wanted to be used by her over and over. He wanted to hear her say "Nod" again and again. Whatever she wanted she just had to say "Nod" and he would obey. That was what he wanted.

And this was how he handled his loneliness, his need for sex, his need for some sort of contact. He happily paid (well it wasn't really his money, was it?) to be used. He managed to find similar mistresses in every city he worked in, even Beijing. He was never happier than being told what to do, or being abused by these domineering women. He never knew quite what to expect, but was never disappointed. Sometimes he was tied helpless to a chair, while the woman teased his balls, or he would be made to simply sit and watch as she played with huge toys until she came, forbidden to touch himself or her. Once he was blindfolded while she described all the things she would be doing to him if she ever took his blindfold off, which of course she never did. It almost didn't matter exactly what the rules were so long as there were rules for him to obey. It was the fact that he had ceded all control to someone else that was so exciting. He was constantly surprised at himself, how he was so willing to be manipulated, to be bullied, hurt even (though he stopped seeing anyone who inflicted real pain on him). He loved the idea that he was there simply to please these women, to be used by them, to be the source of their pleasure and not his own; this was what turned him on. In his business life he was all powerful, he had structured his companies in order for him to be in total control, Boards of Directors were only there to rubber-stamp his decisions, Accountants did his bidding, Secretaries ran to get him coffee or lunch, everyone knew just how important he was; though he went by many names there was no doubt he was the boss. But here in these anonymous and expensive hotel rooms he was a slave, he was the one being used, he was never in control, he was there to do someone else's bidding. And he loved it. He was becoming addicted to it, and he knew that the time would come when he would no longer be able to do this. He wouldn't be able to afford it for one thing. Because soon he was going to give all his money, or actually all of his rich greedy clients money, away. The Philanthropist was soon going to emerge, but he would have to be very very careful now. Secrecy had always been his watchword, but now more than ever before he must be the only one who knew what was going to happen. Tell no-one your plans, trust nobody – these had been his watchwords and they had served him well so far. Not long now and it would be done. His mission would soon be accomplished.

Mogadishu

Mogadishu airport was steaming hot, almost unbearably so. It was only ten in the morning and the heat rising from the tarmac made the planes appear to shimmer as they taxied along to the single runway. No air-conditioning in the private room hired for the meeting, though it had cost enough. Mr. Mackenzie was here to meet a local businessman, apparently an expert in Somalian ways; the British Embassy in Addis-Ababa had been most helpful in putting him in touch with people. Mr. MacKenzie however had not prepared so well, he was wearing a dark suit and shirt and tie, perfect for a meeting in New York or Beijing but far too uncomfortable here. Joshua Mackenzie was a stranger to Africa; he had never been here before and he needed some help and not just with his wardrobe. He needed to know about African law, about African culture and tribal rules, written and unwritten. He needed to understand just how Africans thought.

"Mr. Mackenzie, how pleasant to finally meet you." A slender black hand bearing a single gold ring was extended and, with the merest whisper of a passing handshake, was retracted and folded itself back into the intricately embroidered cool and flowing robes. The smile remained, as if frozen, on the old man's face for the duration of this first meeting.

"Please call me Joshua. And what should I call you Mr. Ndogu?"

"My business clients usually call me simply that, but if you wish you may call me Abder that would be acceptable." A sip of his bitter black coffee and he continued, "I am of mixed parentage myself, my mother was of Arab descent but my father was a native of Somalia itself. Some might say the best of both worlds, but I have struggled at times to be fully accepted by either."

"And Somalia itself is in a sorry state at present, is it not?" said Joshua, his jacket was already discarded but his shirt was sticking to his back and there were dark moisture stains under each arm. He was longing to loosen his tie but unsure if this would be appropriate.

"I am sad to admit that circumstances force me to agree with you Mr., sorry - Joshua." The smile almost cracking into a self referenced laugh, "But even though we are considered by many as almost a pariah state we have still managed to retain our dignity." He stared deeply at this pale white man in a far too warm suit. "We are a proud people with a long and splendid history, much ignored and maligned by the rest of the World, but in a strange way we serve the purpose of being the whipping-boy for the rest of Africa. 'We may be in a mess' they say in Lagos or Nairobi 'but at least we are not Somalia.' You see, even in these troubled times we are able to retain our sense of humour." Abder smiled and wondered at the discomfort of the white man, he too had once worn these ridiculous Western suits when he was a young man, but now he appreciated the cooling nature of the long flowing robes of his native Somalia.

"As you know I have a proposition for you to consider. You have I hope read the papers I sent you?" enquired Joshua with a questioning look.

"Yes, but I do not quite understand your motive?" a pause while he waited maybe for an explanation. None came, so he sipped his coffee again. "You say you are being philanthropic, but I see little advantage coming to our people here, in fact I would go so far as to say that they may in fact find themselves being used, as so many have been throughout these long years. You see, true altruism is even rarer than you might believe and especially here in Africa we are rightly suspicious of Charity. 'Beware of Greeks bearing gifts.' They taught us that at Eton, and though I do not suspect your parentage in the slightest I do detect a touch of the Hellenic in your proposal."

"How civilised you are Abder. And yes, in a way your people will be used. You are correct that nobody gives expecting nothing in return, and I, or rather my scheme, will benefit greatly from the co-operation of your people. Though I can assure you that my companies will be rewarding Somalia in a measured and proportionate way; for every Somalian citizen who assists us, your impoverished Country will also be compensated - in the nature I have already outlined for you,"

"Ah, so now we get to the real point of your business I see. And how much would this 'assistance' amount to exactly?" Leaning forward and glancing sideways (even the walls have ears here) he almost whispered. "We deal here in US dollars actually. Even though all our politicians swear the United States of America is the true residence of Satan himself a surprising uniformity breaks out when those funny little green-backed dollars are waved about."

"That is for negotiation, but I was thinking of one thousand dollars for every signature we receive. This 'investment' would of course be guided by your good self. I do realise that that would put you in a position of some power and an element of trust would be required between us. I have been assured that you are most respectable; but for our part, that trust would be enhanced by total discretion on your part."

"My dear Joshua, I hope you are not trying to bribe me. I am already a rich man and have no need for more money. My religion also forbids me to accept bribes of any nature; not that has stopped many on this continent as I am sure you know." A slight look of disdain crept into his smiling black face. "Sadly corruption is as rife here as in the West, though I have noticed that you are more successful in hiding it."

"No. I am not trying to bribe you. On the contrary, I will have it written into any final agreement that there must be complete transparency as to the final destination of our, shall we call it, "contribution" to the development of your country. I have been informed that you are a good man, a safe pair of hands if you will, and that you will use the funds we are prepared to donate wisely." The heat was too much for him and he slipped the knot of his tie free and undid his collar button.

"I wondered when you would make yourself more comfortable Joshua. And you are correct in your estimation. I thank you. I am indeed a rich man and in fact I would be far richer if I were to move my operations to Kenya, for example, or Ethiopia – the old enemy itself. But I am old now; I have lost the appetite for wealth which drives so many. I am also proud to be a Somalian, and I would like my endeavours, small as they may be from now on, to benefit my own people."

"And I share those sentiments entirely. It is also a sad fact that whenever one attempts to help the most deserving of people, it is usually the middlemen who get rich and the poor who tend to stay poor. I would truly like to change that formula, and I believe that together we may be able to do something to redress this imbalance."

"Noble sentiments indeed. I have gone some way in this direction already. Philosophically I abhor Capitalism, but unfortunately we have to work with it rather than against it." He noticed that his coffee cup was empty and with a small gesture instructed the boy to refill it. "I have, as you must be aware, started a few small banks here. We lend to the young and the clever, and the poor, and most of all – to women. Small scale enterprises which will blossom with the fertiliser we are able to rain down on them. It is only by their own boot-straps that the people here will raise themselves out of poverty, though with our climate that form of footwear would be most inappropriate as I am sure you would be the first to admit."

And so the deals were discussed. The Philanthropist was having the same sort of discussions in Chad and Libya and in Azerbaijan and Peru and in Uzbekistan and rural Burma, or whatever they were calling themselves these days. He was laying the groundwork for his grand act of Philanthropy. The hardest part was timing. Everything had to work like clockwork, and almost simultaneously. As soon as word got out exactly how it worked it could all fold.

Mr. Ndogu was indeed most helpful. This was not always the case, the Philanthropist had to give up in Kazakhstan; he simply could find no local agents who did not want to enrich themselves at the expense of both his companies and the local "volunteers." Elsewhere Joshua was more successful, even if the whole process took far longer than he had anticipated. He found that here in the "third world" certain protocols had to be observed, time-honoured ways of doing business had to be obeyed; trust - that most elusive of qualities takes time to become established. In the West it was barely a consideration. "Was the money there? Were the Lawyers happy? Then sign the damn papers – and make it quick." But here, where it still took days to travel up-country it was as if the world of the internet and computers had still to wait for people to become accustomed to exactly who they were dealing with. Not that they were unfamiliar with the technology, Joshua was surprised just how knowledgeable these "backward" societies were, they simply used it in a different way. It was more important to take one's time than to rush blindly into what seemed such a good deal. Trust had to be established by small steps, and the niceties of each culture had to be observed. But eventually all the pieces of the jigsaw were slotting into place, the required signatures were finally obtained, the papers successfully translated into local dialects and the contracts were agreed and filed in their respective offices. And Mr. Mackenzie duly transferred the monies to starter or community banks where hopefully it would indeed benefit local people. Although of course he had little influence here, the signatures he had, the papers he filed would he was sure benefit many people in Britain.

The first property transactions, or sales, were also beginning to take place. Agents in the U.K. were already negotiating on the properties. No mansions, no grand houses at all. They were simply buying up small family homes, many were ex-council properties that had been sold over the years starting with the Thatcher give-aways and some were starter homes built in the last few years before the prices shot up so high that only speculators and large Landlord companies could buy them. Paul or whoever he was now wasn't really bothered what the price was, though his agents were instructed to haggle and get the best price available. The last thing he wanted was to "spook" the market.

Housing. That was the key. The Philanthropist had thought long and hard in those down-times in that tiny flat in Morden. Housing was the key to alleviating poverty. If you simply gave people money they would spend it or lose it and still be poor, but give them a secure cheap home and they may be able to see a future for themselves.

There was simply no cheap property available in Britain anymore. It had started with Thatcher. Selling off council houses had seemed such a wheeze. Central Government had been subsidising Local Councils for years; but by "capping" their grants from the centre tons of money was released to cut the taxes of the rich, the real wealth generators (or so they thought). And the councils in their turn had to sell off, or give-away really, all that lovely real estate that was just about paying for itself or in some cases cost more in repairs than the low rents were bringing in. And the lucky few who found the money to "buy" their homes made a mint when they sold them again a few years later. Everybody was a winner – and it certainly was a vote winner. Unfortunately nobody gave a passing thought to those who would follow; as the price of housing soared more and more young couples had to give up forever the hope of ever owning their own home (unless their parents helped them, though this just accentuated the gap between rich and poor). And rents in the now almost exclusively private sector just kept rising, couples were forced into renting smaller and smaller flats and resorted to bringing up their kids in expensive cramped conditions which their grandparents had once rented for a fraction of today's prices. When the Tories were re-re-elected in 2025 they completed the job by forcing councils to sell the few remaining council houses to private landlords, who would only buy if they could raise the rents proportionately - so rent controls simply had to go too. Coupled with the abolition of any responsibility to 'rehouse' the homeless and the stopping of all housing benefit (after all why should decent tax-payers give money to these layabouts) many of the poor families were forced into studio apartments or one bedroom flats originally built for singles. Many families pooled resources and shacked up with others, three to a house sometimes. Anything to get a roof over their heads. And misery ensued. Whole generations would be brought up living like rats and their only hope of escape was the plethora of lotteries or becoming a celeb, a porn-star or a football player. Even crime as a career was far harder now, though nobody counted the thefts from fellow poor people. The Police wouldn't even investigate so nobody bothered reporting it, just make sure someone is home at all times and keep the door well bolted and barred.

So, thought the Philanthropist, how do we begin to even solve this? No, solving it was impossible. It had gone far too far for that. Socialism had been tried and had failed in one country after another; as soon as people became better off they started voting for themselves rather than others. He might be able to alleviate the situation for a lucky few, maybe help some to grow up in a decent home, with space for the kids to develop. A small step but one he was determined to take, not because he was some sort of Communist but simply to show the world that it could be done. Changing the world was his motivation, seeing the system defeated if only for a short while, making a mark, and all to be done anonymously, if they ever found out who was pulling the strings they would be cut (and everyone left dangling), he was sure of that. He knew the way the world worked and if he were ever identified they would stop him. So, how to do it exactly? How to improve people's lives and to help them without their own innate greed kicking in and defeating the whole process? He could simply rent out at a "decent" rent the houses he was buying. Why not? There was nothing to stop him setting up companies that would buy properties and make big losses by charging low rents. But he suspected that that might not work. Not in the long term, there would surely be investigations by other jealous landlords. Cries of "foul" could almost be heard before he started. And with those investigations would maybe come the collapse of his phoney house of cards empire, and when that came crashing down the new rental companies would also fold and that would be the end of his bold new experiment. No, he needed something more permanent, something that would take years to unravel, or maybe be simply unravel-able, a tangle so intense that they, the authorities, angry depositors, the banks, who knows but whoever and all would simply be unable to untangle it. He also needed to guard against greed. Just because you were poor there was nothing to stop you becoming greedy. If you were suddenly the recipient of a low-rent home it wouldn't be long before you started sub-letting to other unfortunates and pocketing the difference. So he had to come up with a way of giving away his (but it wasn't really his, was it?) fortune without those who received his largesse simply cashing in and selling out; he had to devise a new way of giving people a home that they could neither sell or sub-let. And he thought he had the answer, complex as it might be.

Bolton

The first family were from Bolton. Sally Richardson had just lost her job at the call-centre where she was being replaced by a computer. Careful analysis had worked out that there were only a couple of hundred possible questions callers might ask, and indeed only about twenty probable ones. It was hardly rocket science to go back and see which answers real operators had given that had satisfied the disgruntled punters. And satisfying people was the key; give them the answers they are looking for, placate them and they would remain faithful consumers. Clever tech now disguised the computer generated voice so that it would alter phrasing and dialect and tone with each new caller. And so Sally was dumped unceremoniously along with fifty others here in Bolton alone; another triumph for Capitalism. It hadn't been much of a job but with her husband John working on the black rubbish vans (unregulated and operated by a rogue but cheap gang-master who paid cash) they just about got by most weeks. They were of course in debt, I mean who wasn't? But they managed the minimum repayments most months, and when they couldn't "GoogleCash" usually extended their credit limit, even if that meant next month's payment would increase by a few Euros. They lived with their three young kids in a former council flat built originally for single people in the 'Nineties', but overcrowding controls had been relaxed in '23 – it had just been too expensive to re-house people - cheaper to let the market decide. And the market decided that anywhere to live was better than the streets; if you had a family there really was no choice, any accommodation, however squalid, however tiny – as long as you could afford the rent.

They had been contacted by local agents who brought them into the quite unassuming office in the nearby trading estate and explained exactly what was being offered. Their own home? Yes, that's right – your own home.

"You mean, like we own it? Really, I can't believe it." exclaimed Sally, this was never even a possibility for people like them; the only people who could buy were landlords or the kids of rich parents.

"Hang on a minute," John jumped in "We could never afford the repayments; Sally has just lost her job. We don't know when she'll get another one. Or even if she will, she were on waitin' list for two year for that one and now that's gone, there's nout out there for the likes of us that I can see."

"You won't have to make any re-payments Mr, Richardson, we are effectively giving you the house." The agent said in his quiet reasonable manner.

"What do you mean, giving us the house?" John Richardson exclaimed. "You must want something in return. Nobody gives some-at for nout."

"You are generally correct Mr. Richardson, may I call you John?" the elderly agent explained. "But in this case you are mistaken; you are indeed being given the house. And technically for nothing too, or practically next to nothing; call it an act of Philanthropy if you will, but somebody is really prepared to give you something for nothing. You are actually the first of many, and I do understand your hesitancy, but really there is nothing to fear. There are however one or two conditions you will have to fulfil and I must enlighten you as to those."

"I thought so." said John, there were always conditions.

"Shut up you idiot, and listen." Sally desperate to calm him down interjected. "John, the man said he was giving us the house, and nothing you say will stop me taking it. I can't live in that tiny flat any longer. Let's at least hear what these conditions are, and then we will decide. Just don't blow it by getting all aggressive." And turning to the agent she said politely "Go on please."

"They are quite simple. The house will to all intents and purposes be yours, no-one will be able to take it from you. You will be given a lifetime lease (that is for both of your lifetimes) but this will not be transferrable, even to your own children. When the last of you dies, a long time in the future we hope, the property will revert back to its true owners. But you will live rent-free in this house until then. In effect you will be sitting tenants who pay no rent. But the house will never actually be yours, though your right of tenancy will be secure for your own lifetimes. To all intents and purposes it will be yours, but not to ever sell or sub-let or make any financial gain from. It will simply be a decent place for you to live in, think of yourselves as caretakers if you will – because you will be expected to maintain and decorate the house. The person giving you this property will also expect you to obey certain rules. And should you not agree to them or if you break the covenants of the lease, let us call them the conditions, then the lease will be broken and the property given to someone else. Is that clear?"

"Aye, but let's hear the conditions first." John could still not quite believe that anyone was giving them something for nothing. The

Philanthropist would soon be in the news and everyone would be dying to be a recipient, but the Richardsons were the first couple, theirs was the first act of Philanthropy.

"Exactly. We must all be clear on that. You will be signing a lifetime lease but before that, and after this meeting if you agree to proceed, you will be having a meeting with an independent solicitor who will be paid for by us but who will give you unbiased advice. That solicitor will also explain to you in more detail exactly what the conditions are and how they will be monitored, but monitored they will be, so you must be sure that you can adhere to them before we proceed."

"Let's hear the conditions then." John knew it was a scam, he had been conned before.

"They are in fact not onerous at all. There are three main conditions. One is total discretion, you must not divulge any details of the lease or your meetings with myself or any other representatives of shall we say "The Philanthropist" who is giving you this property. Secondly you must not sub-let or in any way attempt to borrow or raise money on this property, and thirdly you must live in this house for the rest of your lives. If you vacate the property the lease will also expire. Surely these conditions are not so unbearable as to stop you from accepting them, are they?"

"No. We are both Bolton born and bred, I wouldn't want to live anywhere else, would you John?" and the look in Sally's eye was enough to shut John up. That look meant she had made her mind up, he knew that look of old.

"No, that true. I just can't quite believe it, that's all." He sat there stunned and slowly the possibility congealed in his mind to a reality.

The Philanthropist

"Would you like to see the property first? Or would you rather have that meeting with the solicitor we have arranged for you." the agent said, holding out the keys to them.

Our friend was watching through an internet link, and couldn't stop an involuntary lump from rising in his throat as he watched the incredulous but happy smiles of Sally and John Richardson, his first ever couple.

The Philanthropist had started slowly, buying houses at auction through small property companies he had set up, one here and another there and for a while nobody suspected anything. The houses were renovated using small local tradesmen, and people were moved in with little ceremony. But a few estate agents had begun to ask questions. Why were the properties not re-advertised for sale or for rent, who had handled the sales or lettings; no-one they knew? And nobody knew who these small companies were, were they charging rents and if so how much; how would that affect the market generally? And then when enquiries were made at the Land Registry the awful truth began to emerge. The houses were not sold on, and just 49% was actually leased to the new joint 'owner/tenants' for just £100. And the companies retained the deeds. No rent was demanded, just a silence from the recipients. A promise not to speak to the press, which lasted for a few weeks in most cases, but you couldn't expect people to keep quiet forever, could you? But by then the purchases had accelerated and houses were being scooped up wholesale. It soon started a stampede of sellers desperate to cash in, and the inevitable happened. The price of houses started to fall, as lemming-like millions all rushed to market. Then sure enough the prices began to rise again as others, worried that houses couldn't stay this cheap for long rushed to buy. The Philanthropist simply upped his game and bought and bought and bought regardless of the price. He had armies of agents already set up and his own conveyancing teams waiting for his command to buy, the money had been in place for months, all cash purchases and no questions asked. It had never been a ploy to lower or raise the price of houses; that was an incidental, of no consequence to the Philanthropist at all.

It had actually been an attempt to change the nature of ownership itself that he desired. For centuries the only options were to own or to be a tenant (at the mercy of your landlord) of some sort. Now within a few short years there was a large proportion – estimates vary but possibly as many as fifteen percent – were living as lifetime leaseholders and paying no rent at all. He was quietly re-arranging the world, though this time the clamour would be deafening.

Well it couldn't go on forever. Within just five years The Philanthropist had bought and effectively given away more than six million homes. Something had to be done. After an initial fall prices were rising again and pretty damn fast too. No-one was certain what would happen next. Would these Philanthropic companies (no-one was really sure if a single person was behind it all) keep on buying whatever the price? Would the value of houses become meaningless? The Prime Minister had to act, if only to stop the uncertainty. And so the sale of houses was suddenly stopped. A moratorium was declared. No more houses could be bought or sold until a full inquiry had taken place. But by then the damage had been done. As ever the Governments response was too little and too late. Over six million homes had been effectively given away. Rents in the almost exclusively remaining private sector started tumbling. Potential tenants were understandably holding off; who knew, they could be the next receivers of The Philanthropists largesse. Private landlords were crying all the way to their mortgage-holding banks who didn't even want the wretched houses back – they couldn't sell them now, could they? But the landlords couldn't find tenants either; the market had largely collapsed as millions moved into their new £100 homes. Any landlord who still had tenants was busy reducing the rent – at least some money coming in was better than nothing.

And millions were instantly lifted out of poverty, had a decent roof over their heads, had no mortgage or rent to pay, and for their whole lifetimes too. A huge saving; a few just sat around watching screens and spent the saving on booze, but several really grasped the opportunity and started small businesses or tried to get better jobs or saved for their kids futures. At least, and at long-last, they had their self-respect. It was large businesses that were the most furious. So many had diversified into property – there was no way they could lose – until now, that is. This was simply unfair; our whole system was built on the free market; supply and demand deciding prices, and here was a lone individual suddenly flooding the market with cheap property. Or worse than that, he was actually giving property away; how could anyone determine the value of a house now? It went against the whole idea of the market; this was plain stupid. It simply couldn't continue, heaven knows where it would end.

And there were angry questions raised in the House. This was bordering on Anarchy. It was simply ridiculous, and couldn't continue or where would we be? What about all those who had saved for huge deposits and were still paying mortgages? How unfair was it on them? And the banks were suffering too, demand for new mortgages was non-existent – why take out a mortgage when you might be given a house by 'The Philanthropist' soon. And then when the moratorium was introduced a lot of people stopped paying their mortgages altogether. They couldn't sell their houses now, and the banks wouldn't took them back because they couldn't sell them either, so why keep on paying for an asset you couldn't sell? And who knew when the moratorium would be lifted? The inquiry would take forever, and what it would recommend nobody knew. And then many of the property companies began to stop their loan repayments too, I mean it was unfair – why should a blind eye be turned to private mortgagees and not to them. So the banks were in financial trouble again. Central Government had sworn never to intervene again; in fact they had passed legislation to allow failing

Banks to be absorbed by other Banks in an orderly fashion. But this was different, this had never been foreseen; all the banks were in trouble and nobody wanted to buy them, and the UK banks had all borrowed the money to lend for mortgages and to business from Banks in other countries, and now nobody was repaying their debts. The IMF was scared of contagion and so the Bank of England was forced to step in and "lend" vast sums to the banks again. History has a tendency …

And all the time the Philanthropist kept on giving houses away. It seemed that no-one could stop him. His agent property companies that had negotiated the purchases were short-lived and all closed after a couple of years, the houses leased out but no company now responsible, nobody could find the company directors, they had simply vanished into thin air, as of course had the Philanthropist himself.

And the investors in his Ponzi schemes were suddenly not being paid their too-good-to-believe but too-good-to-ignore dividends. The Philanthropist had stolen their money to buy the houses; of course he had been stealing their money to pay the ridiculously high dividends for years now. Phones were ringing unanswered in empty offices, letters returned unanswered and e-mail accounts deleted wholesale. The offices were all closed, the staff made generously redundant and in other jobs by now. Some went looking for Mr. Mackenzie or Mr. Greensmith or any of the other aliases but no-one could find him. Private detectives drew a blank, the bastard had simply disappeared. It seems it wasn't his real name anyway. So what was his real name and how do we find him and get my money back? Henchmen were sent to find him but similarly drew a blank, the Philanthropist had told nobody about his scheme, his plans existed in his own head only; and so nobody was talking no matter how much money was offered, they simply knew nothing. The companies accounts had been deleted from the few seized computers, staff who had worked there had been paid off and knew very little anyway. All their communications had been by e-mail, they had never met this Mr. Greensmith.

The Authorities were desperate to put a stop to the giving away of houses but they couldn't decide just which laws the Philanthropist was actually breaking. Then it dawned on them that it hadn't even been his money he had used, but the 'investments' of the super-rich. This was now far more serious and no longer a matter for the Police. Even some in the Government and the Establishment here in Britain itself had been investors. Something had to be done. But the intelligence services were as puzzled, they could easily take this Philanthropist down (nothing could be simpler) but they would have to find him first. And no-one knew where or even who he was.

The Official Government Inquiry was largely window-dressing, it would take years to write a report and by then it would be too late. The lawyers had been consulted but, as far as they could see, the companies giving away the houses had broken no existing laws; someone would have to prove exactly whose money they had stolen first. The Financial watchdogs too were unable to see how anything actually "illegal" had been done, except using someone else's money that is (but actually that is how all financial companies worked anyway). But there were no laws to stop people giving money away and until it could be proved just whose money it was they couldn't act. And many of the super-rich didn't dare report the theft; questions might be asked as to where the money had come from in the first place. And so it was given to MI5, under the auspices of a National Crisis, and within weeks several of the Philanthropists business premises were mysteriously burgled and their computers were stolen. What did they expect to find? Nobody actually knew, they just wanted to catch the bastard responsible. But they found very little, most of the Directors had been aliases too, everywhere they looked they drew a blank.

Our friend, "The Philanthropist" was one step ahead of them all and a few months earlier he had stopped recruiting any new investors, and had resigned (or his proxies had) from all the major Investment Companies he had originally set up. He had successfully, and via many complex transactions through Swiss and Chinese and Carribean banks, transferred billions into the smallish enterprises buying and giving away the houses. He had used a different identity for each Investment Company, and besides he had rarely actually ever been seen, even by the few genuine board members, who were only too glad to be appointed to such well paid positions. Then the problems really started. There was no-one to transfer the vast sums around and suddenly one by one the Accountants running them realised they were heading for the rocks. Who did we now call on for funds when we couldn't pay out the huge annual dividends to the investors? Shortfalls had always been filled without question from other companies, inter-company accounts were huge but no-one seemed to question it as long as the money kept rolling in. But suddenly there was no new money coming in. The huge holes in the balance sheets loomed ever larger.

Meanwhile in the small flat in Morden he watched the news showing Governments in full-blown panic propping up banks all over Europe and America as a veritable financial tsunami was hitting them again. Had nobody learnt lessons from 2008 or 2020 for that matter? Apparently not. As the rich had continued to get richer they had all sought out better ways of making money. It was like a disease. The more money they had the more they simply had to have. Property had been good for a while, and then it had been China and India, but they had both run out of steam too. As for Russia, forget it. Old man Putin was holed up in Moscow with tanks on his lawn and his finger poised on the button; meanwhile his country had long gone to the dogs, there was famine and dire poverty but still he kept his little coterie of lapdogs well fed and though a few areas had broken away and staged their own "Revolutions," (inevitably replacing one tyrant with another) no-one dared to challenge him in his own backyard. Internet bubbles had swollen and burst, new markets had risen and fallen and still the greedy had sought out even bigger profits.

In fact of course our Philanthropist was not the only one running Ponzi schemes, he was just by far the most successful. Worldwide interest rates had been kept low for far too long and Greed had to find an outlet somewhere. One by one the rival Ponzi schemes folded. Even the news reporters tired of reporting them. His companies were the last to go. But go they did, and there was a stream of furious "investors" demanding their money back. Insisting on seeing Mr. Wilcox, or Peter Jones, or Stephen Dalton, but none of these people worked for the various companies anymore. They were referred to Administrators who couldn't really help them but promised to get back to them as soon as this mess was sorted out. He had cleverly tried to insulate them from each other, but when contagion strikes it is almost unstoppable. Dominoes have a habit … He couldn't care less. In fact it was better this way; he could never have stood a chance trying to hold it all together. And that had never been the point. The reason he had succeeded and so well and for so long was that he wasn't greedy himself. He reckoned that all he had spent on himself had been a few millions, all that jetting about and suits and hotel suites had cost a pile of money, but he would have earned that as salary if he had ever actually been employed. He had bought his one asset, his Morden flat outright from the money he got when he was made redundant all those years ago. He had also bought two other small flats nearby and could just about manage to live on the rents from those. He was nearly eighty now and his work was almost done.

He was just putting back the latest Dylan CD (amazingly though dead these last ten years they kept finding new recordings) on his shelf when he heard the knock at the door. A quick glance at his watch, eleven-thirty at night. Ah, so they must be here. In a way he had been expecting them for days.

Paddington

He was interrogated in a small concrete room with a rubberised table and plastic chairs. Cameras and microphones were in all the corners. And one wall was a huge mirror, the Philanthropist new that on the other side he was being watched and studied, every gesture, every facial expression being analysed by faces unseen. This had been where all those Muslim 'terrorists' had been questioned, not that anyone bothered with them anymore now that Greater Iran had brought "Peace" to the entire Middle East. The bunker was four floors down while up above passenger trains brought thousands of visitors and commuters from the West of England into the heart of London, none of them ever guessed that 'The Philanthropist' who had filled so many column inches of newsprint had at last been discovered, not that anyone would be seeing him any time soon. A constantly changing team of five fired numerous questions at him, he simply smiled and stuck to his story.

"I live simply, I have told you that already. I know nothing about all these names and companies you keep bandying about. Look, I am nearly eighty – I haven't worked in years. I live on the rents from my two flats, as I told you. I know nothing about buying or giving away houses. You must have me confused with someone else."

"Mr. Wilson, we know who you are. We know a whole lot more about you than you maybe even do yourself. We just want you to co-operate with us. We aren't here to prosecute you for any crimes. We aren't even sure you have committed any, except impersonating dead people to manipulate companies and steal vast sums of money of course." The chief interrogator wryly remarked.

"But I know nothing. I have told you that already." His hands opened and sure enough they were as empty as he tried to make his mind.

"All we want to know is where the money came from?"

"What money – I have very little money." He knew he couldn't keep repeating the same story but what other one was he to tell; the bus journey to Edinburgh, the homeless years? Now that might surprise them.

"Well, for several years you, under the name of James Pilkington, were paying your ex-wife Fiona maintenance for your daughter Eleanor. At least two hundred thousand pounds a year, by anyone's standards that is rather a lot of money, just what rents were you charging your tenants for your two flats?" The interrogator smiled, surely it would soon be time for him to open up; he couldn't keep this game up much longer. "Where did that money come from? Your solicitors, who handled the transactions, simply tell us that every month funds came into their Client Accounts, regular as clockwork. We just want to know where that money came from."

"Oh that. I made a few clever investments over the years." He tossed off half-heartedly, knowing it was just playing for time.

"We have your bank statements Mr. Wilson, or should we call you Mr. Pilkington or Mr, MacKenzie come to that? That money came from several numbered Swiss Accounts which we cannot at present access, but we will as soon as the legal hurdles have been jumped over. Would you care to help us? It might speed things up a bit, and your co-operation will be appreciated. Or rather your lack of co-operation will be noted." The veiled threat behind the smiling face. "So, would you care to help us out here?"

"No. Not really." And then smiling too he played his last card, "But there might be a way I can assist you."

"And what way would that be?"

"Well maybe we can make some sort of a deal." said the Philanthropist.

"Sit down Paul. I may call you Paul? That seems to be your longest lasting alias. Is that okay?" another day, another interrogator, this time a middle-aged woman, on her own this time and quite attractive too.

"Sure, as names go it's as good as any." He replied.

"We may as well call you Paul. Paul Wilson at least has been around for a couple of decades, unlike most of the others." She looked knowingly at him over her horn-rimmed glasses.

"Okay, for now I am happy to answer to Paul."

"Well, this is a fine mess we have here, isn't it?" She was smiling, as if talking to a five year old.

"I wouldn't call it a mess at all. A re-adjustment I might describe it as. Even a "come-uppance" springs to mind." He smiled back, in a way he was enjoying this. He knew it would always come to this and he had had years to think about it. Not to plan his defence, he had no defence, but to give his side of the story, his version of events.

"Look Paul, let me be frank. I quite admire you in an abstract way." Again that knowing smile, complicity was worth a try. "But I am a representative of the state and as such I am here to uphold the security of that state. Personally and in my humble opinion the country has been going downhill for years now and maybe we needed someone to shake things up a bit, but whatever my private opinions I am not employed to have a view on that, I am here to protect the state, whatever state that state might be in, if you can excuse the pun."

"Agreed, and as that representative you are here to stop me. Well, I have stopped. I have finished my little game, my attempt at re-distribution; my acts of philanthropy are over. The Philanthropist has no more money to give away, but you have probably guessed that. But more importantly I think you may find it rather hard to undo all that I may have achieved." He smiled back at her; letting her know that deal or no deal he wasn't going to be a pushover.

"We know that you have stopped, you are here in our custody now. And my, our, task was never to stop you, but to deter others. To make sure that nobody pulls a little stunt like yours again. Our job here has mostly been to keep an eye on discontents. The powers that be have been scared of a revolution for a while now. We thought that by taking Russell Brand down for kiddie porn we had put a stop to those ideas, but others, far cleverer too, jumped into his shoes. We have been stopping them one by one. They were amateurs mostly, but we never suspected an attack might come from our own side, from among the rich themselves, and you Paul were one of those no matter how much you might plead poverty now. The Government has known for some time that they had to change. Even the rich and powerful know you cannot squeeze people forever, they just didn't really know how to turn things around. If only we could get back to how things were at the turn of the Century. And frankly, even the Big U.S. Corporations that were driving the whole show have come to realise that they are running out of options. The more they automate and save on wages the fewer consumers able to afford the products they used to make. There are less poor and desperate countries left to exploit, nowhere else to export poverty to. If I sound like a revolutionary I am only repeating what has been common knowledge in Government circles for years. There has been a growing realisation that really another way should be found. I, and those who work with me, owe our loyalty to whoever is running the country, but we also know that what we think you have done may not be the worst thing to have ever occurred. In some ways as I said I quite admire you. We just need to know exactly how you did it?" The friendly head mistress looked at him in a knowing way.

"So you can stop others I presume." The naughty pupil replied.

"Oh, I think there is little danger of that now. Things are beginning to get back to normal again. The banks are being re-financed and the housing market will be allowed to re-start again soon. Everything, every single purchase is on-line now, and we can and do track every financial transaction so it would be very hard for anyone to replicate your actions. The banks are technically all owned by the state now, we can see if anyone tries to emulate your actions pretty quickly now, and we are putting in controls to try to make sure it doesn't go crazy again, though most of that chaos was down to your activities I am afraid."

"You flatter me. All I did was act in a way the so-called free market found inexplicable, and their greed did the rest." Paul replied.

"That's one way of looking at things, I suppose. Look, let's cut to the chase. We will not be prosecuting you. I am prepared to put that in writing." She confided.

"What a pity, I was quite looking forward to my day in court, exposing all the greedy idiots I took the money from." The Philanthropist said.

"And that is exactly why we will not be prosecuting you. Don't you think they have maybe suffered enough – losing their money like that?"

"It was their greed that lost it for them; I was simply the conduit for that. If it hadn't been me it might have been someone else. And I do not shed a single tear for them. Not a single one, not even the Foreign Secretary, did you know he had that much cash stashed away? Most of their money was stolen from someone else anyway, if you go back far enough."

"Possibly. Quite possibly, but we will never know. Most of them will simply go away and lick their wounds I expect. Far fewer have come forward to report your theft than you might expect. What concerns us more, is how we deal with the people you have re-housed, your leaseholders?"

"As far as I can tell, and of course we had our lawyers prepare those leases very carefully, they are totally legal. And as you have probably discovered it will be virtually impossible for you to ever find the actual owners of the properties."

"Yes, that was indeed a master-stroke I must say. Each property is, we think, owned by hundreds, if not thousands of individuals, peasants, herdsmen, whatever you want to call them all over the third world."

"I thought that might make things a bit difficult. Unless you pass retrospective legislation returning the property to their 'rightful' owners, but we are pretty sure that indigenous people all over the world will then demand that they too have their lands returned to them; and Britain was the country that stole most of it centuries ago too. It could get quite complicated. I think the best thing would be to just leave things as they are. In fact I don't think you can possibly undo those contracts, even if you wanted to."

"So you think we should just let it be. Leave all those lucky people to live the rest of their lives in houses that were bought by stealing the money from the super-rich?"

"Exactly. That is what I set out to do, and I don't think you really want to undo it. You said earlier that you or your political masters were scared of a revolution. So you should be. And if you confiscate, illegal even though it would be, these properties you could well trigger one. In fact I think this should act as a salutary lesson. Your masters should realise that they must begin to redress some of the inequalities in what is left of our society before the shit really hits the fan." He said smiling at his interrogator "Treat this whole episode if you like as an extremely messy fart."

"Paul. I have told you already that we will not be prosecuting you. But we can make what remains of your life very uncomfortable. Nobody knows you are here, and I am sure that nobody cares. Nobody will miss you when you are gone; you've made sure of that yourself actually by your treatment of everyone who ever came close to you. Why don't you co-operate? Tell us what you know, or what you can remember. Just so we can dot the i's and cross the t's. The press as you know have dubbed you "The Philanthropist" and nobody has a clue just who you are. In fact you may consider yourself rather lucky that we found you and not the henchmen of one of your victims. If you think we are unkind you might have had to redefine what you might have called brutality. Some amongst us actually advocated feeding you to them. You must realise that none of this can ever be revealed. No-one will ever discover the identity of The Philanthropist. No-one will ever know how you did it. It will always remain a mystery, and believe me; in the scheme of things it will soon be forgotten. Tomorrows chip paper, as they used to say, as you too will be; forgotten - as the next earthquake or Royal baby takes centre stage. You have had a good run but the ship of state will sail majestically on, leaving you and this whole debacle far behind in its wake. I must also tell you that you will never be allowed out of confinement again, that goes without saying. We can't have you discovered now that we have gone to the trouble of finding you, so you will spend the rest of your life as our guest. But we can make that confinement very comfortable or very unpleasant. Which would you rather have?" that knowing smile again, she took off her glasses and folded them in front of her.

"And what is there to stop you from simply taking me out and having me shot when I have told you all that I can remember?"

"Nothing at all. You will just have to trust us. But even we do not shoot people lightly. You are an old man. What would we gain by shooting you?"

"I suppose I really have no choice, do I?"

"No, I don't think you do? Let's call it a day for now. We can start properly tomorrow. And may I just say Paul, I am so glad we could see eye to eye at last. I look forward to what you have to tell us. It is quite a story I imagine."

And so the Philanthropist told them everything, or most of it. To be honest there were things he forgot, details that eluded him. He had long ago burnt the famous blue ledgers. His own computer had been dispensed with months ago too. But in the end they got almost everything they needed to know. It had taken weeks, going over and over the details, the investors, the amounts, the multitude of companies, the fake directors, the property companies and the aliases. He was tired, he just wanted to sleep. It had been an exhausting process and had taken several weeks but at last it was over. He had succeeded. His act of philanthropy, his manipulation, his changing the world around him was over. For now he just wanted to sleep, his work was almost done.

He was woken at five, though he didn't know what time it was. His watch and the bedside clock were gone.

"Wake up Paul, it's time. Put your clothes on and come with me."

And they took him into a small courtyard. He couldn't see the sun yet but he noticed that dawn was just breaking; the sky was a lightening blue. Somewhere he could hear birds singing but as he looked up they were nowhere to be seen. He was asked to sit in a chair and just then he felt the edge of the sun as it touched his face. It warmed him and he smiled inside. He knew what was coming, the final act of Philanthropy. They shot him.

Printed in the United States
By Bookmasters